Grace and Ease

AN ASCENSION MANUAL LIGHTLY VEILED
WITHIN A TIMELESS ROMANCE

J. G. LEVEE

Copyright © 2022
By J.G. LeVee
All Rights Reserved. Athens West Productions LLC
No part of this book may be used, reproduced, or
distributed in any manner whatsoever without the
expressed written permission from the author.
www.SedonaPsychicHealer.com

The scanning, uploading, and distribution of this text via
the Internet or via any other means without the permission
of the publisher is illegal and punishable by law. Please
purchase only authorized electronic editions, and do not
participate in or encourage electronic piracy of copyrighted
materials. Your support of the author's rights is appreciated.

Book editor, Bridget Armstrong
Cover Art by Damonza
Author Photo by Alex Lockett

ISBN-978-1-958586-10-5

CONTENTS

Acknowledgement v
Voyor's Soul Group vii
Voyor's Character Matrix Map ix
Prologue xi
I wonder... xii
Pre-Life locker room xiii
World-Side xv
Chapter One: ...she replies, "No words!" 1
Chapter Two: "Maybe it's Karma or something!" 12
Chapter Three: "Starmark? What's a Starmark?" 34
Chapter Four: "The first and most important truth is that we are choice!" 43
Chapter Five: "I've chosen to be 'born with a veil'!" 55
Chapter Six: "I sure do like little miracles!" 69
Chapter Seven: "...You are strong with the gift." 83
Chapter Eight: "...getting old doesn't serve me." 101
Chapter Nine: "I'm talking about a spiritual relationship not a worldly one." 113
Chapter Ten: "...I Will be the Hell and Measure of your Faith!" 128
Chapter Eleven: "Shouldn't we be choosing our scent?" 139
Chapter Twelve: ...'the logic of emotion' 148
Chapter Thirteen: ... "Your now is nearly here..." 159
Chapter Fourteen: "Now what?" 180

ACKNOWLEDGEMENT

I wish to express my profound thanks to Bridget Armstrong, for noticing and nurturing the small flame that became this novel. Her willingness and perseverance to see this work from start to finish reflects strongly on the soul she chooses to be. I also give thanks to Todd who would not read the work without a character map as his guide.

I also wish to thank the seemingly endless line of souls that tried to convince me to give this endeavor up. As with all investments, this novel would not allow itself to be cast aside and was an excellent opportunity to practice keeping my eye on the prize.

Finally, I give thanks to Spirit for guiding me through the trials and tribulations of channeling this work through the veil at four in the morning.

VOYOR'S SOUL GROUP

Voyor's Soul group, like all others, is composed of seven souls including himself. As a group, they can take advantage of playing different roles in each incarnation to further the understandings required to accelerate their group and individual ascensions. The following character descriptions are offered to guide the reader's journey as we follow Voyor's growth.

They are presented here with their soul names in italics and their Earth-bound names in brackets [World-Side i.e.WS]. A Character Matrix Map is also provided to show the inner relations between Voyor and his Soul Group.

Lowe is Voyor's best friend and a bastion of trust. [Jonah, WS]

Freemar explores the art of choice as [Chance, WS] with a few twists and turns planned.

Lor is the kindest and gentlest soul and will take the form of a massive male named [Manson, WS] in her efforts to explore power.

Kara, the seer, known as [Zune, WS], reflects the moment the veil came to be and how that can affect us.

Lorna, the keeper of Truth, prefers blind justice.

She has chosen to take the form of [Marshal, WS] a male who will serve as Mara's assistant in her early and mid-career.

Mara is the first soul that Voyor was ever privileged to see. Her eyes clearly show a reflection of her elegant complexity. With over two thousand lives lived between them, Voyor and Mara are both on the brink of their final ascension. Her perfect name to use as a banner is [Grace, WS].

Pre-Life is guided by many levels of *Seniors*. Seniors are souls that have completed their ascension but choose to assist other souls on their journeys.

Also, note that the story is anchored with a few constant threads. The most notable is that of looking in the mirror. That act helps us measure the overall state of character growth within the world.

VOYOR'S CHARACTER MATRIX MAP

Pre-Life Side (Character Names)	Character Focus	World-Side (Character Names)	
Voyor	KNOWING	Ease	Fear Possibilities
Jade	PASSION	Leah	Passion Twist
Mara	GRACE	Grace	Endless Love
Lowe	TRUST & Service	Johan	Best Freind
Freemar	CHOICE & Fate	Chance	Twist & Turns
Lorna	TRUTH	Marshal	Black & White
Lor	POWER	Manson	Gentle Power
Kara	SEER	Zune	Part of Mystery
Senior	GUIDE	SPIRIT	All Knowing

Unexpected Substitution Twist before Last ascension — arrows from Jade to Lorna

ix

PROLOGUE

Just a moment ago...

Wow, it seems like just a moment ago I was soaring through the universe. My mind was free of concern and my heart was brimming with love. Turning, floating, and flying, free of the pain and loss of the planet I'll be using as my platform for mastery. Good old Earth. I know you well my friend. I've walked your paths and swam your streams over a thousand lifetimes and still I call upon your support once more. Such a magical place you truly are. You support our whims and deeds. You, good Earth, hold our space and make everything a race as we long to find our light again...

I WONDER...

I wonder where I'll live this time
I wonder how fast I'll grow
    I wonder how I'll meet you again
    I wonder how we'll know
        I wonder if this will be the last
        of so many lives we've lived
            or can we jump to another time
            a place for us to give.
                And in that moment before we are
                In the stillness of our light
                    May we feel the warmth of visions past
                    and this time, make it right.

PRE-LIFE LOCKER ROOM

From an earthly perspective there is a moment between being light and being now. A beautiful moment when fellow souls join in sharing, planning, and prepping for the next in a series of lifetimes designed to support our ascension. We call this special moment that reflects all our hopes, dreams, concerns, and fears, the Pre-Life locker room. Like the many sport events around the world, each of us simply wants to get in the game and make a difference. That is so with me! I currently call myself Voyor and have returned to Pre-Life with my soul group in hopes of completing our joint ascension.

As I look around Pre-Life, I see a magical reflection of the earth into which we will be born and continue to grow. It allows us to understand, clarify and plan the special moments and interactions between members of the soul group. It is a system that has supported our growth through the corridors of time. It is the paradox between fate and choice. It allows us to have a plan and still be free to choose how we embrace that plan.

As with all good systems, Pre-Life is guided by many levels of Seniors. Seniors are souls that have completed their ascension but choose to assist other souls on their journeys. They appear to each of us differently but always as a well trusted friend. So, it will be with me and my soul group as we consider that this could well be our last life to live…

However, we have much to plan in a short amount of time. For even the moment between the clock's ticks is just that, a moment. Pre-Life is also a semi-veiled state of being. It's a place where I can remember the whole of my journey but not that of my fellow soul group. This allows each of us to be genuine with each other and recreate ourselves anew. No baggage for us in this here and now. There will be more than enough time for that once we're World-Side. Then, only our intuition can serve to guide us if it's guidance we seek!

WORLD-SIDE

With each passing generation,
Earth has paid the price...

Streams once flowing at a graceful pace
are now clogged with human waste.

Skies once blue and filled with air so clean
now color our sunsets and disguise the scene.

Her resources taken with no concern,
wisdom offered but none earned.

I hope I soon can show the way
to bring us back to the light of day.

And in that light, we'll know to be,
one with Nature all of us free...

CHAPTER ONE

...she replies, "No words!"

Pre-Life: On the way to a session

THE MOMENT HAS passed, and I find myself walking down a luminous corridor. I look to my left and see an infinite field of stars just beyond the corridor's windows. They glisten and dance as each, in turn, glows bright and dim within a larger wave of energy. I laugh to see the reflection of the densers around my ankles and wrists designed to modify my base frequency. I'm still not used to the latest setting but know all is on pace for my entry point into World-Side. I arrive at a portal marked Lerner Level 3 and enter. A group of six other souls already sit around a table in the center of the space and talk among themselves.

Pre-Life: The soul group

The first soul to catch my eye is Lowe. He has been my best friend since the beginning of our time. He is steeped in the ways of trust and has instilled a foundation of those qualities to the entire group. He has evolved his Pre-Life form into that of an athlete. Strong and sure, his presence always allows me to explore the edges of my spirit with confidence. He plans to assume the name Jonah in the coming life and serve as my best friend. My heart is in awe of my love for him. Yet he rarely asks for anything in return. From my point of view, there is none more qualified to be at my side.

To my right sits my new growth partner, Freemar. Like the gambler on a streak, he has explored the art of choice from the very beginning. For the most part, Freemar has been very passive as a guide to my understanding of fate vs. choice but that is all about to change this time around. Incarnating as Chance, Freemar has planned a few twists and turns but will not share the plot with me. It's all for the best. For how could I embrace my choices if I already knew the results? That would be no choice at all!

To my left sits Lor. She is the kindest and most gentle soul I have ever experienced. If one were to touch the smallest of flowers, one would just begin to understand how her love inspires all beings to grow under a welcome sun. She, like I, have played many roles on our way to mastery but none will challenge her like the one that awaits her this time. No more being soft for her! This time she will take the form of a massive male named Manson in her efforts to explore power. A brute from the start, he will be passionate to inflict grief on me at every turn. It's amazing what we do to climb the ladder of ascension.

I exchange glances with Kara, the seer, who's wide-eyed and always present. From the moment the veil came to be, she has explored the reflection of its mysteries. This is the first time that she will be part of that mystery and not just extend her abilities to see through. She has chosen to incarnate as Zune and will serve many of us as we rekindle our intuition and knowingness on World-Side.

Next to her sits Lorna, the keeper of truth. She, like blind justice, has been impassioned from the beginning to make truth the fabric that supports all exchange of wisdom. By my timeline, she is but a Halfling with only about 500 lives lived. Her form seems to reflect her desire in the way her hair falls wildly about her shoulders and down her long form. She stands as a bridge that spans the great rifts between perception and fact. Still, she is of the notion that there can be no middle ground in searching for the truth of a situation, but that's why we're all here, to grow and expand from understanding to knowing. With our last World-Side experience being that of husband and wife, Lorna has chosen to take the form of Marshal, a male who will serve as Mara's assistant in her early and mid-career.

And finally, I look upon Mara, the love of my being! Since the very beginning of our creation, Mara was the first soul I was privileged to see. Her shell is far more refined this time as her eyes clearly show a reflection of her elegant complexity. Her long body is sure, yet still able to respond to life's race. Her grace and being has continued to stir me in ways beyond want, beyond need, and beyond love itself. When I look at her, I have no edges, no sense of me, but rather only we. She too shares this space of "me and we" and has chosen to guide her expansion as a complement to mine. With well over two thousand lives lived between us, we are both on the brink of ascension. This turn of the wheel waits for us! So, in the moment between plans and lives, I am taken with all she is and all that we can be. She is gentle yet firm in her longing to know how old souls may transcend all the roles and find their hearts are truly one. She has yet to select the perfect name to use as a banner on World-Side, but I know it will be perfect to reflect the being that is truly her!

Pre-Life: The session

The Senior motions me to join the group and I take the last seat. As his joy surrounds us, he calls, "Come my friends, join hands, and bless this moment for all it is and can be!"

We join hands and immediately experience a charge; a surge; a flow of energy into each of our beings. It's a pulse and a knowing of each soul in the circle as a whole and yet as separate as snowflakes on the first day of winter. As I scan my soul for a yet deeper level of knowing, I feel a surge of energy fill my hands. I begin swaying to and fro to a rhythm unheard. My heart pounds to the point where I must open my eyes. Directly across from me sits Mara. I am taken with the knowing that we are joined! I've heard of links like this before but had never thought or understood the moment. We smile at each other as our bodies sway, all the while the other five souls remain with eyes still shut. This knowing seems to go on far beyond my sense of time. Yet her smile is not new to me. Still, I have never gazed upon her as I do in this moment.

Senior now asks each of us to share our experience. Most of the others noted senses of one type or another. I tasted this. I felt that, until it came time for Mara to share.

Still looking at me she replies, "No words!" At that point, I know that she is speaking from her heart not her head. I had, in preparation to being, pondered words, words, and more words to reflect the feelings still racing inside me! So as the question is asked of me, I laugh, smile, and agree with Mara, "No words!" Now this is the first time I have ever been at a loss for words but at the same time I realize that words could not serve me now. Not with this pulse. Not with the beating of my heart in time with the ebb and flow of my being and hers.

Pre-Life: Beginnings and contracts again

I don't recall what happens next until Senior introduces the session topic. "Today we'll begin your World-Side contract list. As you know, this list will guide and mark your path as your soul continues to expand. Note too that these contracts will affect most, if not all, your major interactions while on the material plane. Let me give you an example. We have all learned about the journeys of Lerner. Let us study one."

I'm very excited about anything to do with the tales of Lerner. He feels so very close to me in so many ways. Just the mention of his name sends a shiver up my spine.

Senior opens a viewport with a wave of his hand to display a timeline web of threads representing Lerner's many lives. Senior scans the web and selects a single thread and expands it so we can see a series of dots. Each dot highlights major and minor crossings with other souls. Senior points to a large red point and expands it into a scene within the viewport.

Pre-Life: Past-Life with Lerner

The scene opens with Lerner dressed in Renaissance clothing and riding a horse through a grassy meadow. Suddenly, the horse is spooked and rears up, throwing Lerner to the ground. In a nearby field, a servant had been busy tending to the planting of the crops. At the sound of the horse, she sees Lerner fall, drops her bag of seeds and rushes to his side. Lerner is dazed as the servant carefully lifts his head.

"Are you all right, my lord? Can I help you? Please, my Lord, do not move just yet for you have fallen!"

Lerner looks up into the caring eyes of a common maiden but is unable yet to see. Suddenly, from the field, comes the angry voice of the field's keeper, "Wench, how are you to be there? What manner of care do you give the field when the birds have all but eaten your measure of seed?"

In fear she replies, "But my lord, I came to the aid of this soul who's fallen from his horse. I am sorry, my lord. But please allow me a moment more for he is not yet fully with us."

The keeper now enraged shouts, "Return to your planting at once! I will attend to this soul."

The maiden gently lays Lerner's head on the ground and reluctantly returns to her planting.

A moment later, the keeper helps Lerner up and to his feet. "Are you all right my lord? How is it that you have fallen from your horse on such a fine day as this?"

Lerner still dizzy, looks around slowly and speaks, "I do not know my friend, but I am in your debt. Please accept a token of my appreciation for coming to my aid."

The keeper looks back at the maiden and then to Lerner as he slowly accepts three pieces of gold and returns to the field. Lerner brushes himself off and moves to remount his steed as the maiden looks on with relief.

On top of his steed, Lerner notes the keeper yelling at the maiden. As he continues to watch, the keeper strikes the maiden, and she falls to the ground! The maiden struggles to gather the remains of her spilled seed. For a reason foreign to Lerner, this act of violence feels unjust, as shown on his troubled face. We hear the thoughts of Lerner questioning, "How can this be? What manner of deed can bring on such rage?" After quickly dismounting, Lerner approaches the keeper.

In the next moment, he grabs the keeper's hand before he can strike the maiden again. "Hold Keeper! What has this servant done to receive such pain?"

Angry, the keeper shouts, "My lord she neglects the field, drops her seed and strays at will!"

Lerner looks first to comfort the maiden by offering his hand and gently lifting her face as he pushes the keeper away. "Dear soul, how have you come to this pain?"

The maiden looks back in silence knowing her words will bring anger from the keeper yet again! Seeing this, Lerner directs the keeper away and asks again of the maiden about her actions.

Softly she speaks, "A thousand pardons my lord. I was only trying to help you after you had fallen from your horse. I was afraid for you. In rushing to your side, I dropped my seed and strayed from my task."

In a flash of knowingness, Lerner smiles and gestures for the maiden to stand. "Fear no more my dear one, for your care goes far beyond the field I see. Yet your keeper fears your heart as he should. For it is indeed great, beyond fear of his hand! Please take my hand and join me as I ponder."

The maiden slowly rises and follows Lerner as the keeper moves forward to object. "Where are you going with this maiden? She is charged with planting of this field."

Lerner turns to the maiden and asks, "Dear maiden if you would be so kind as to give your seed to this soul so that he may begin to learn what you already know."

With wonder, she hands over the seed still unsure of her situation. The keeper, equally unsure, takes the bag.

Lerner turns to the maiden and asks, "Who among you holds care and understanding of the seed and the seasons?"

The maiden replies, "Willow. She is gifted in knowing such things."

Lerner calls out, "Willow, come to me for I am in need of a favor." Willow curiously approaches the group. Once there, Lerner asks to see her hands. She presents them to him. It is obvious by seeing her calloused hands that she is truly a servant of the field. Lerner smiles and removes Willow's sack of seed and hands it to the keeper. From the keeper, Lerner removes the sash of station and places it upon Willow.

All are at a loss as Lerner tells Willow, "Please dear keeper, share your knowing and love of this field that all may grow a bit stronger with the passing of time and ensure that this new soul finds the joy in sharing not only his own, but the burdens of others."

The old keeper moves to speak but instead hears Lerner say, "No words will serve you now! Enjoy your gold and allow the bounty of your actions to give you counsel in this next year and a day." All are silent as Lerner and the maiden walk away and Willow begins to instruct the old keeper in the ways of the land.

Pre-Life: Back to the session

Senior freezes the moment and proposes a question to the group, "What are the contracts in play from that moment?"

Freemar eagerly raises his hand only to have Senior remind us, "Contracts are timeless and should earn a bit of reflection!" We all close our eyes and breathe into the moment as we have been trained countless times.

Slowly, after the emotions of the group have passed, Lowe offers, "I feel that the maiden was in disrespect of the keeper and compromised his charge. Maybe he was wrong to hit her but considering the time-period that would be normal."

Senior asks, "Additional comments?"

Kara adds, "I think it was not really about the maiden at all, but rather an entire event designed to allow Willow to take charge of the field. I bet if we followed Willow's timeline, we would find that she might have changed the entire health of her tribe with her knowingness of the land."

Senior waves his hand to highlight Willow's timeline and then moves it forward two hundred years. We see her great granddaughters sitting in counsel. One speaks of giving grain to nearby tribes during a regional famine. Senior waves his hand and returns to Lerner's moment and notes, "Very good, Kara. Anyone else have a comment to share?"

As I sit and watch the discussion continue, I can't help but wonder about the maiden's choice to come to Lerner's side even though she knew she would be punished.

Senior pauses for a long moment and then says, "With love my dear souls, you all have presented a perspective of merit that defines the value of the moment. Continue to reflect a bit further and we will discuss it again soon. As for the remainder of our time here, have any of you developed a contract you wish to share with the group? Remember, you are an active soul group or in your case, soul pod, with a clear band of interactive potential!" Senior turns to the star-view and looks out. "Remember too, that the stars reflect the gates you share. One simply needs to pass through them." With his last words Senior phases out of the session space.

We are all quiet for a while and then begin to leave. Lor notes how he'd already missed being able to phase but was getting used to a new setting on his densers. I also feel a bit uncomfortable on level seven. I long for what seems just a moment ago to be again within all!

CHAPTER TWO

"Maybe it's Karma or something!"

World-Side: Jonah and the rock

JONAH HITS MY window with a rock. I could keep time by it! Yes, like always, it's 7:07 a.m. He hasn't missed a morning in years. He's crazy! I remember two years ago he had the worst flu and he still snuck out, threw his rock, saw me in the window and ran back home to rest. I don't know how he does it, let alone why. As always, I go to the window and there is my best friend Jonah with a smile on his face and ready to embrace the day. I open the window and shout, "Hey bro, what's happening?"

He always replies, "You man. Hurry up! We're going to be late!"

In the next moment, I throw on yesterday's clothes and am out the door and on a hero's pace to school. Walking with Jonah is not for the weak of heart because he's never been late for anything in his life. So, if you want to hang with the big dog, you'd better be able to run.

As usual, Jonah asks me if I studied for the geometry test. I laugh, "No! Why do that when I just know the stuff."

That's one thing that Jonah hates about me. He doesn't get that stuff at all. And to top it off, he can't figure out why we study it in the first place. It doesn't matter though. If he wants to play ball, he's got to get the grades.

World-Side: Manson again

We're almost to homeroom when Manson spots us in the hall. I don't know what his problem is, but he always seems to want to kick my ass.

Manson yells, "Hey jerk, get out of my hall! You know the drill. Wimps use the back stairs or pay the price!"

Jonah moves between us and says, "Chill, Manson. You need to find someone else to harass!"

Manson barks, "I got no beef with you Jonah. This is between me and Ease!"

"Look Manson, like it or not, if you got a problem with Ease, then you got a problem with me. So, let's move on."

Determined, Manson replies, "Forget it, Jonah. Someday you're not going to be around, and Ease is going to have to fend for himself. It might as well be now!"

"Not now Manson. Not now. Not ever! And just what makes you think that Ease might not just kick your ass?"

Manson smiles, "Good point. Let's see it. Come on Ease, bring your best shot!" Just then the homeroom bell rings. Manson shrugs, "Damn! Saved by a friend and the bell again! Your time is coming Ease!"

As we walk away Jonah turns to me and asks for the hundredth time, "What in the world did you do to that guy? He's on you every minute of every day."

Shaking my head I reply, "Nothing in this world! Maybe it's Karma or something!"

Manson stands at six feet four and weighs in at two hundred and sixty-two pounds. As a football lineman, he is noted to be cruel on the field. In the world, he is almost always feared. But for me, he is simply hell! Since my first day of school, Manson has made it a mission to fill me with fear. Yet, through this torment, I have gained my dearest friend in Jonah. I remember back to that very first bus ride when, at the age of six, I was so excited to share my joy and toys. I still to this day don't know what I did to provoke him, but I did. I remember him saying, "Give me that toy," as he grabbed it out of my hand. I didn't know what to do!

Just then, Jonah stepped between us. The stage seemed set and the roles cast for a scene we would continue to play out again and again, yet within me is a hope for change. Something has got to change. I just can't do this anymore!

Pre-Life: Change of plans

Lor and I walk through campus like we have for thousands of World-Side years. We always make sure to visit any new additions or changes to the landscape. It's a chance to see the inventions and styles that will appear during our next incarnation. Today is especially exciting because we get to see a mature communication network called the Internet. It's still quite crude in terms of spirit but it will serve as a reflection of networking that we call intuition.

Lor puts her arm around my shoulders and laughs, "Hey Voyor, what's up with you and Mara? She's got you lost in your heart."

"It sure seems that way. I don't know what exactly changed except maybe everything! How about you?"

Lor thinks for a moment and declares, "I've turned my densers down to level six and wow it's almost too much to bear."

"Why'd you do that? We aren't to shift densers for another four pulses."

"I know but you'll never guess what happened."

I look at her for a moment and then pause to calm my emotional field. I begin to scan her top to bottom to top again.

Lor laughs "Stop that! I didn't ask you to scan me. I asked you to guess."

"You caught me! But you're too late. I'll bet another window opened up for you."

Lor smiles, "Man you're good. How did you know?"

"It was easy. I noted that your first and seventh centers are a bit more open. Your seventh would seem to mean more possible expansion, while your first would be another shell opening."

With concern Lor adds, "Voyor my friend, I feel so torn but feel I must leave the group."

I stop suddenly to look at her face as she says, "I have chosen to take a walk-in which will place me three years ahead on the timeline."

I feel a sinking feeling in the depths of my soul. We have played out roles together for the last hundred incarnations and this is hopefully going to be our last time on World-Side!

She continues, "I do, however, have an idea of how we can complete our contract. Rather than being brothers again, I propose we birth into unrelated families instead. We will not even grow up in the same area. Instead, I'll step in and grow up in an environment that focuses on physical anger and envy. You'll grow up as planned with Lowe at your side as Jonah. He will serve to dampen my rage in all cases as part of his study of trust and service."

I ask, "But how does this help our process? I really need the power to master my fear of possibilities. I spend way too much time considering what might happen instead of being present! Even worse, I get so wrapped up into possible futures that I actually attract them!"

Lor says, "I know. I know. But hear me out. This approach will empower you without me at your side.

The plan is simple. I'll be driven to hate you. The very sight of you will drive my envy. You will represent all that I long to be but am not. Again, Lowe as Jonah will hold space between us and expand his field of trust. This sets the stage for you to feel my rage and reposition your reaction patterns. At some point, the constant badgering will drive you to action! You will have no choice but to be present with confronting me versus fearing the worst. Even better, you'll relieve Jonah of his duty of service. Finally, you and I will stand face to face, thus allowing you to be fully present. In that moment, you can choose to fully commit!"

Pre-Life: Choosing to be a walk-in

Allowing her words to sink in, I reply, "Lor, you're amazing. You have a gift my friend. But tell me, was I right?" Lor looks around a moment to make sure we are alone. In a quiet voice she says, "I could have a real chance at taking this walk-in!"

"That's amazing and rare. How many times have you successfully executed a walk-in?" Lor reflects, "I've attempted seven but only two have worked completely." Concerned, Voyor comments "It doesn't sound like very good odds. What went wrong with the other five?" Lor shakes her head and reflects, "It sounds like a simple task, but it's far more complex than you'd think.

First you must find a receptive soul that has come to an impasse in their own ascension. That in itself very rare. Then a physical compatibility study is required to understand the advantages and disadvantages of the new pairing. Sometimes the original owner has badly compromised the shell so much in their frustration that it only is able to support the walk-in's intention for a short while. Other times, the original owner succumbs to a highly addictive pattern which also compromises the walk-in's agenda. But the very worst situation comes into play if the original user changes their mind and attempts to regain control of the shell. It is in that moment when the shell begins to exhibit a bipolar outward appearance from the world's point of view.

In that case, the shell radiates a feeling of mistrust from all parties and severely limits the agenda of the walk-in." Voyor counters, "So, why do you think this time will be any different? It feels like a huge risk!" Lor smiles, "One simple reason, I know where and when this shell has been. It's been used as a template by many of our soul group for countless incarnations. It will be like reconnecting with an old friend."

A bit relieved, Voyor asks, "When did you find out? When will you know?" Lor replies, "Just a few sessions ago. One of the Guides took me aside and shared the possibility. With all the planning our soul group is doing, this seems very odd to me."

"Odd is an understatement. What about all the other contracts we've been working on together? Not to mention the contracts with the other members of the group?"

Lor adds, "You're right, we've been pooling and planning for hundreds of years to complete this tapestry and now this shows up at the eleventh hour. It just doesn't make sense. Yet I feel strongly about this opening. As for the others, they're clear. You are the last one I needed to talk to."

I yell, "I'm the last one! What's up with that? How many times have we chosen to be brothers, lovers, and every combination under the stars?"

"That's why this is so hard. But hey, let's focus. I've been the power at your side for a long time and now it's time for you to be your own source of power. The bottom line is our remaining contract. Tough love is just one aspect of Yin and Yang that we explore to find the middle."

"Okay. Give me a moment to clear so that I can hear you." With that said, both of us raise our hands to center our emotional fields. Our color changes slowly from a red hue to more of a violet core with bands of gold.

Once there Lor begins, "I love you more than my mind will reveal to my heart, dear friend. You are and will forever be a part of my process, my core, my being! And as part of that love, I long to see you be free! So, as Manson, I will look on you with different eyes and find respect for your commitment…"

World-Side: Today's the day

I woke up today feeling a bit angry. I'm angry at myself for being afraid. I'm angry for all the time I've wasted worrying about something and someone I can't change. This anger keeps growing. It's growing bigger with each passing day. So today, somehow, I'll change my life and find a different way.

I meet Jonah on the way to school like every day of our young lives but somehow, it's not the same at all. Normally, as we would get closer to school, we would always plan how to slip by Manson. Today however, I don't mention it and neither does Jonah. Sure enough, like clockwork Manson finds us in the hall.

I look at Jonah and say, "I'll see you in homeroom. I'll be all right. I'm so done with this!" The emotions of my heart seem to roll around in my head. I'm tired. I'm empty. I can't feel the fear anymore. I have, for the first time in my life, sent Jonah away so that I might now begin to explore.

Looking Manson in his eyes I speak, "Okay Manson, I guess it doesn't really matter when we do this. It's got to be done! Who knows, maybe I'll do a little ass kicking along the way."

I focus even more intently into Manson's eyes and prepare to fight. The scene seems to be slowing down in time. I'm different somehow. I feel my heart racing yet have no time to think. The past is gone. The future is yet to be! Every cell in my being is in the present moment. And with that, Manson sees the fear leave my eyes.

In the next moment, Manson's rage begins to flow out and away from him to be replaced by an uncertain and new respect of commitment he now sees in me. Manson sways a bit, postures a bit, and finally drops his hands with a nervous laugh saying, "Wow dude, you're really ready to rumble. Sort of takes the fun out of the fear game. I guess we better get to homeroom. I wouldn't want to get detention for a fight that didn't happen!"

Pre-Life: Lor's replacement Jade

Voyor looks deeply into Lor's eyes asking, "You would do this for me no matter how long it takes?"

"To the end of time and back my friend!"

With that, I have a sense of joy knowing I have contracted a plan to empower myself while at the same time contributing to my friends. We knowingly walk into the grand hall and down a corridor in joyful silence.

Lor finishes walking me to my next session and bids farewell to me and the rest of the pod group. A bit reflective, I take one of the two remaining chairs. Although my head understands Lor's opportunity, my heart is in a place of loss. Further, my soul begins to form a void of sorts as I glance at the empty chair beside me.

Senior phases into the room and is joined by Jade, Lor's replacement. Jade sports a slender yet strong shell and moves with an unassuming grace. She is thoughtful and focused on herself and the group at the same time. A power currently beyond the group seems to radiate from her and fill the chamber. Jade is of course in the process of refining her beingness to our group priority. We all do the same regarding the signature she brings to us. After a long moment of silence, Lorna requests an opportunity to speak.

Senior nods and Lorna addresses the group. Lorna begins, "I'm a bit concerned about the mastery Jade brings regarding the topic of trust. I feel that she has possibly over-assumed her level of mastery."

Knowing how passionate Lorna is about truth, we as a group are not surprised. Jade, on the other hand, is visibly and energetically affected. Senior raises his hand and suspends the emotional charge that has begun to fill the room. Calmly, Senior asks, "Lorna in what way are you concerned?"

Lorna responds, "I'm feeling like she believes that trust is a process. How can trust be anything but black or white, Senior?"

"Good question. Let us speak to this. Jade, please begin."

Jade stands to address the group, "I have committed twenty-four lives to this topic. I have explored each facet of the trustee and trusted and present the following current conclusion: Trust is not a channel one should or really can offer. Rather, it is more like a progressive contract that grows and expands over time. In the simplest of terms, I choose to trust no one, but am willing to give all souls an opportunity to earn my trust. Further, it is vital for the parties to establish a constant channel by which they can communicate." Lorna asks, "What do you mean?"

Jade continues, "A channel consists of three aspects. First, one must get our attention. Second, one must keep our attention. And finally, one must share some information that both parties consider relevant and true. Without that foundation no truth can ever exist." Lorna reacts, "Isn't that a given?"

Jade goes on, "Now, picture a bar filled with lots of souls just looking for an opportunity to share. In comes a female dressed very provocatively. In that moment most of the males in the room will respond with a turn of their heads. The female now has a subset of interested males from which to pursue. The next challenge for the woman is to keep the desired male's interest. This would fall into the category of flirting. Finally, the woman is charged with the task of finding a topic that the man considers relevant and true. To continue moving forward, the man is also required to find a topic that the woman finds to be relevant and true. At this stage, if either party fails to maintain each other's interest then the focus is broken and both parties return to their previous patterns."

On face value, that is an unexpected position and quite foreign to our group's current understanding. Senior encourages Lorna to continue.

"I don't see. Is not limited trust, no trust at all? Is not the entire goal of our ascension that of being fully one with all?"

The group looks at one another for some sense of understanding as I stand, and Jade and Lorna take their seats. I state, "I am beginning to expand beyond my former notion. I absolutely agree with Lorna that the end-goal is always about the whole, but I believe that Jade speaks of the process of transitioning from where we are: A place that is neither here nor there; a dynamic state that is and must allow for the presence of mind. Not that that's my strong suit!"

We all laugh at my comfort and willingness to jest at my personal challenge to be consistently in the present. The mood of the entire group now moves from caution to consideration. I add, "If I, as a soul, have just understood a truth about being physical, that does not mean that I am yet a master. It simply means that I have an understanding and can attract opportunities that match that understanding. I cannot, however, offer an opportunity to interact as a master. In that way, Jade's approach offers both compassion and growth. This seems a bit more loving than the trial by fire that Lorna is so fond of."

With that said, Lorna thoughtfully adds, "Thank you Jade. I have an unexpected growth in my heart and soul today! I must say that I love the black and white of truth but as Voyor pointed out, you must get there first."

Following the tradition from ages past, we all raise our hands to form a circle of flow to celebrate our new-found collective understanding. There is something truly special about unexpected growth. In one minute, you think you live a truth and in the next you are in wonder at how your entire world has changed.

Pre-Life: Garden of Harmonious Light

In the next moment, I am in the Garden of Harmonious Light. Wow, I must have crossed a flash point! Each time a soul in Pre-Life is on the verge of a bit of mastery, we shift from the moment we are in, to a place and time between moments; an opportunity to reflect on the topic in a quiet and guided way. This is indeed one of those moments. Light flows everywhere in patterns that change from snowflakes to the pulses of my beating heart.

Souls pass me one at a time, in pairs, and sometimes in groups of three. I wander over to one of the fountains to watch more closely how their energy fields interact with the water and each other. Wow! Just look at that soul. They're almost fully embraced in a red hue. From my memories that is quite rare to see here. In what has only been a moment, their hue now seems to be draining away from them and into the nearby pool. Still further, in no time, the pool has returned to its original shade of blue. Water is one of the universe's most dynamic gifts. It allows us to change our state of emotional being in such a smooth and gentle way.

Oh look, there is another couple coming toward me. Their auras look as if they are linked together at the first and fourth. I wonder what that means. From behind me a gentle voice says, "They have chosen to be joined in soul and body."

Chosen to be joined? Darn! I'm certainly not very present as I turn to see Senior standing behind me.

"What do you mean, 'They have chosen to be joined'?" I ask.

Senior replies, "Each of us, as you know, is on a journey to enlightenment. In the larger scheme of things this would require each of us to experience each and every aspect of being to complete such a journey. This is where the magic begins! Now let's look at the two souls we see here as they move on their journey. Each, if being faithful to themselves, will continue to explore and expand in their own perfection of choice. Let's say for simplicity's sake that each soul has one hundred units of beingness to master. In the first moment they meet, each has mastered fifty units, or half of their goal. Of the fifty units, each soul has twenty-five units in common."

I'm thinking this is a word problem.

Senior laughs, "Patience young one, allow yourself to be present. To continue, soul A has twenty-five units of unique wisdom from their journey and twenty-five units of shared mastery. The twenty-five units of shared wisdom can serve as a foundation for understanding. Remember that they share the mastery of twenty-five units but not how they got to that mastery. This foundation now sets the standard of exchange. It is vital to understand each other's approach so that we can be aware of how each one processes and filters new data. The way each of us discerns the difference between truth and perspective."

Suddenly, I realize what Senior is saying, "Oh, I get it! Perspective is everything! I was just in a session…"

Senior lays her hand on my shoulder and calm falls over me. My words are replaced by the vision of the couple sitting across from us. Senior says softly, "Now watch closely young one. Look to see small orbs of knowingness flow to the space between both souls. As each begins to slowly move across to the other, they change color and shape. Finally, once within the other soul, they melt into the whole of their spectrum."

By simply observing the process, I'm increasing my own mastery of understanding this topic. Of course, with Senior's hand on my shoulder she is transferring data to me in a similar way. From her however, I needn't be concerned regarding perspective. For to be a Senior a soul must have transcended all notions of perspective as a basis of truth.

Without saying a word, I hear Senior in my mind saying, "Yes young one, we are joined. Feel my presence. Feel the absence of perspective. Feel my being. We are one."

I, with no luck, search myself to know where she ends, and I begin. This is almost the same kind of feeling I had with Mara, yet different. With her, I felt more about expanding and now I feel more about knowing.

Senior smiles and says, "You're correct on both counts. Mara has much to share regarding your heart space. Here, we are sharing a knowing about the process of sharing. Now let us conclude our moment. As you can see, knowingness sharing is based on an understanding of the souls that are sharing. The beauty is that we can and do expand with every sharing! It is for us to glean the difference between perspective and truth. That, however, is its own session. May you effortlessly be in your now, Voyor."

Pre-Life: Back to the session

With her last words fading in my mind, I find myself back in the paradox session. Senior knowingly smiles at me and asks, "Is there anything you would like to add, Voyor?"

On their own, words come out of my mouth seemingly as I say, "Overall perspective is vital for our final mastery but understanding each perspective is equally important for us to gain clues to the truth. It's like a beautiful mystery. By knowing what a given perspective is, we can begin to understand the whole more quickly and therefore will not need to experience the other soul's journey!"

As the soul group processes my example, Senior adds, "Well done." Senior then poses another question, "Is any single perspective more useful to our understanding than another?"

The group is silent as I calmly share, "The only one in this case is that of observing the moment as a whole. It is from this perspective that we can both allow and honor each single perspective with no weight given to any specific one." As the last word leaves my lips, I'm enveloped in a blue orb of light.

Pre-Life: Master moment

I see my soul pod, yet they no longer see me. I sit before a master adorned in a robe with electric blue trim. She sits floating before me, and her presence fills me with peace. She speaks directly to my mind with heart-felt joy, "Be calm young one. You have grown much in the passing moment! You are no longer to study within the paradox sessions, but rather join in the articulation team."

I think, "What does the articulation team do?"

"The very reason you sit before me is the result of the example you developed to explain paradox. With each passing generation within the world, we must reinvent our ability to convey such wisdom and understanding. Your offering will serve the world well. I will share with you from time to time as you grow further in this field."

Pre-Life: Back at the session

My fellow souls look intently at me as Senior stands to address the group. He bows to me and says, "Voyor will no longer be joining this session group as he has owned a truth."

My session mates feel a variety of emotions about

the statement. I feel Lorna scan my being for clues of my new insight. Mara projects a wave of love. I can't help but focus on the giving glow of love coming from Mara. Her light almost blinds me with a sense of selflessness.

With the session over, the group slowly moves to leave. I continue to bathe in Mara's light as she approaches. I'm motionless and cannot speak. She gently smiles and softly asks, "Perhaps you might be willing to share a bit of your new mastery with me soon?"

I want to yell, to jump, to laugh but do none of those things. I feel so weak as she gracefully moves away.

World-Side: Ease after school

Wow what a day! I confronted Manson and didn't get my ass kicked! Jonah seems a bit relieved by the whole non-event as well. It seems like he had been attending more to being trustworthy by protecting me than living his own life. But hey, that's what friends do, I guess. I must say however, that there seems to be something more to our friendship. I just can't quite put my finger on it.

On a fun note, I aced the geometry test with flying colors. It was so weird. I just look at the problems and my mind goes into space mode. It's like I don't need to try. More like remembering facts instead of learning them.

Matter of fact, trying doesn't work so well. I just stare at the shapes, and they start moving around on their own. What's even funnier is that my head doesn't step in when I get an answer. It just goes on to the next solution. Man, sometimes I come up with three or four answers in the time it takes the class to get one.

I couldn't help myself today though. Jonah was tanking as we were about ready to exchange papers and grade them. So, I knowingly asked the teacher which of the three solutions I found for the last four questions will be used for grading? Poor Teach turned red as the class ignites into a unified protest about the unfairness of the questions. Having no recourse, Teach throws out all four to the cheers of the class. We do have another test on Friday, but I bought us all a bit more time. And to top it all off, Manson comes up and high-fives me. Go figure. How does one go from being bullied to becoming a hero all in the same day?

World-Side: Geometry lesson

Jonah comes over after dinner to work on the geometry for Friday's test. I love geometry so this is fun for me but not for Jonah. As he likes to say, "Ease, you make my head hurt."

So here we are again, like so many evenings, working on the books instead of pounding the latest video game. Tonight however, I have a new plan! Tonight, we are going to forget the details and go for the process. I start by asking Jonah to share his process saying, "Just tell me everything you're thinking as you think it."

Jonah looks at me with a laugh and says, "Everything? You mean every detail? Ok, here goes. To start with, why do I have to do this stuff? I'm never going to use this stuff in real life!"

I stop him right there, "You're making this really hard on yourself already and we haven't even started! Understand that emotion is a powerful field of energy, and you just allocated a ton of it to fuel your fire."

I continue, "Ok, let's look at this from an energy usage point of view. Let's say you're on your way to anywhere and you have ten units of energy. Now let's see what needs energy. Ok, your head needs energy to steer. Your car needs energy to run. You'll need a bit of energy for the tollbooth. I think you get the idea. In this case, using any energy for emotion doesn't get you the answer. Even worse, it continues to distract the rest of you from getting the answer. So, work within a Zen space. Clear your mind of anything and everything."

Jonah does his best to comply. With him in a calmer place, I ask him to look at the problem one aspect at a time. This time, I tell him to note each item as a known or unknown. Jonah moves through the aspects as I keep asking, "Known or unknown?" In a moment, we're done with that step.

Jonah seems a bit calmer than usual now, so I continue, "Ok you're the football guy. Think of the unknowns as the defense and the knowns as your blockers. First, let's take on the simplest unknown.

Now which of the knowns relates to your guys that can touch the defender?"

"Oh, I get it. Who relates to who?" In a moment, he reduces all the unknowns down to two.

Getting excited myself, I say, "Now comes the magic! Use the newly defined knowns and apply them to the last unknowns. Remember, do the easy problems first."

In a moment, Jonah stands on the brink of his solution with only one unknown to solve. His focus and new process now move him forward. "I got it!" he yells. "Yes, I did it! Me, a math guy."

In short order, I watch Jonah dive into the next problem and know he'll never be the same. Giving him the answers was never part of it for me. It's about empowering him to find his own answers that rocks my world!

CHAPTER THREE

"Starmark? What's a Starmark?"

Pre-Life locker room: Starmarks

We finish our first flow circle with our new groupmate Jade when a nova streaks across the viewport of our session chamber. I yell, "Wow, that would be a great Starmark."

Jade looks at me and asks, "Starmark? What's a Starmark?"

Freemar, our guide of choice and chance, stands and shares, "A Starmark is a signal or tool we use to navigate our contracts and growth. It's similar, in a basic way, to mile-markers on a road in World-Side. In this case, if your car breaks down or you need to give directions to someone, you just reference the last mile marker you passed to tell them where you are. In the case of Starmarks, it's sort of the opposite. When a Starmark appears, it can mean one of two things. First, it can represent a star point of a contract between two souls. In that case, both souls become aware that an interaction is afoot."

"And the other case?" Jade queries.

Freemar continues, "The other situation is an 'Ah-ha' moment when a soul reaches a new level of understanding or mastery."

"I still don't get this. How do I know the difference between a contract interaction and an understanding?" Jade asks, puzzled.

We all smile and say in unison, "You don't!"

Freemar continues, "That's the beauty of it. If we know which is which, then we negate our opportunity for choosing. And to make things even more fun, a single Starmark can mean both an interaction and understanding. That's my personal favorite!"

Pre-Life locker room: Soulmates

"One more thing, you said future interaction of a soul contract and not one that has already occurred?" Jade asks, for clarification.

Freemar replies, "Yes. Think about it. Suppose you and one of the others within the soul-group creates a contract to be mates in a given lifetime. It's as they say in World-Side, that 'love at first sight' thing. The 'you're my soulmate' thing!"

The whole group, including Senior, laughs while Jade wonders what's so funny.

I add, "It's not you Jade. It's one of our favorite

myths of World-Side. The soulmate! It is one of the classic distractions to affect the heart center as we explore within a lifetime. So much effort is given to the notion that in a lifetime we have only one soulmate, when really, each of us has six."

A perplexing look comes over Jade's face. Freemar continues, "Think for a moment of how our sessions are organized here. You study with six different groups of six. Now in any given group, there are two souls common to multiple groups. Let's use our group as an example. Senior, would you share a visual example?"

Senior waves his hand and seven golden coins appear on the table. Freemar stacks them up and says, "Note that all the coins are the same size." Then he picks up the coins and places one on the table. He points to the single coin and says, "This represents Voyor. This group centers around him. This is his soul group or pod."

Freemar now carefully positions the other six coins around the first coin so that they touch each other and perfectly surround the first. Freemar adds, "When we incarnate into our next lives, any of us are his soulmates in that lifetime. Whether male or female, young or old, and any race under the sun, we are his soulmates. Now Voyor is also a part of six other groups in which each of us is the center. So, in that case he is one of our soulmates."

"I still don't see what's so funny," Jade interrupts.

I turn to her and say, "Jade, while in World-Side let's suppose I first cross paths with Lor, and she is also a male like me. As my first encounter on a soul level, I might interpret my intense feelings for him as love and conclude that I must be gay. At that point, I might sway my entire life perspective and priorities to serve my connection with him. Then, say I meet you, Jade, incarnated as a female. Now you are also in my soul group which would lead both Lor and me to wonder about being gay since we both are equally attracted to you and to each other."

The group giggles a bit as I continue, "So now what are we: gay, bi, straight or what? Depending on our contracts, we might hang together, break one of us off or taint all our views of love in the process. The bottom line is more about allowing each of us to experience a soulful connection rather than trying to fit into a world convention of relationships and in doing so, miss many opportunities to expand." With pleasure Voyor states, "At this point in my growth, I stand before you with the understanding that I don't require myself to react each time my body, mind, or heart makes a request of my soul. It's all about the process of choice!"

Jade's eyes get big as she absorbs all that is being shared and asks, "Will you join me in a flow circle again?" Her request brings a wave of love over the room. We all smile and join hands.

I look to see that Jade is finding peace with the new information when Mara's and my eyes meet again. Our shared energy seems to lead the group as it grows into a loving shade of lavender.

"Just one more question," Jade interjects.

I love Jade's passionate enthusiasm but wish I could hold the field with Mara a bit more as I say, "Sure, what is it?"

"We have never been soulmates before or even part of the same soul pod. Why now? What's changed?"

I respond, "You've changed. I've changed. We've all changed. As we continue to grow and evolve, we, each in our own time, move closer to the center of beingness. And with that movement, we become more bonded with more and more souls. In the purest sense, when each of us arrives at the true center of being, then at that moment, we share the soul pool of the one. There we will pass beyond the notion of soul pools all together! We are then in the place of one and one is all!"

"Will I be your next choosing of a soulmate in our next incarnation?"

I look at Mara and then back at Jade saying, "I don't know that yet. Perhaps. Perhaps not. For me it's not about new versus familiar. I have yet to contract with you or Mara or anyone in the group. However, I do know that as each life passes, we continue to evolve, and our attraction becomes stronger."

I look away from Jade and into Mara's eyes and then return to Jade. "Again, in the purest sense, if Mara completes her half of all wisdom on her journey and I the other half, we will then set the stage for a joining of perfection!"

My speech seems to slow as I again turn slowly to

lose myself in Mara's gaze. The whole group, except for Jade, knows of Mara's love of me and my hope of her.

The smiling Senior adds, "Focus Voyor. Back to the present my dear soul."

I refocus my gaze back to the entire group and continue, "Yes, perfection is a perfect union of souls where the divine masculine and feminine become pure knowingness. In one moment, the process of discovering each other's wisdom, in the next moment a part of oneness beyond measure. I feel so very close to it. It calls to me! It is me! And I'm sure that soon we will all know being…"

World-Side: So much stuff used to define self

Wow, college! Classes don't start for two days but I just had to get here early. As I look out my dorm room window, I see my fellow students scurry about unpacking cars and saying goodbye to tearful parents. It's a perfect day with the sweet scent of autumn in the air. I go about taking the last bit of stuff out of the last box. Wow, moving sure is a pain. Why, or rather how, did I get so much stuff? I thoughtfully ponder as I remove my high school diploma from the box. Should I hang this up or trash it? I certainly don't need this but why can't I seem to just dump it? What's this all about? I feel funny like I should know something. I just don't know what.

World-Side: Falling like never before

A young woman I've never seen before walks in through my open door saying, "Hey there, is this Roy's room?"

Totally taken by surprise the diploma slips from my hand and I dive to the floor to get it. Wow, just in time, I save the diploma and turn to see a stunning soul with an angelic voice. She seems to have an aura of gold about her. Yet I am caught within her wild gaze.

Leah laughs at me flat on my back with the diploma grasped tightly in my hands. I reply, "Roy? Maybe. I just got here. I really don't know who my roomie is yet."

A moment of silence fills the air as we look into each other's eyes. A sense of knowing comes over me but of what I am not sure. Finally, words return to me as I say, "More importantly, who are you?"

Still laughing, Leah says, "Hi, I'm Leah. I've never had someone fall for me as I entered the room before."

Trying to save face, I respond, "I'm Ease, and I didn't fall for you. I just caught my diploma from falling on the floor."

"Is that a college diploma, Ease? You look like a freshman to me. I mean this is a freshman dorm!"

Still waffling, "Look Leah, I am a freshman, and this is my high school diploma."

"And why would you have that here? That is so last year my friend. Here you'll pay your money, and they'll give you a nice new diploma at the end of four years to replace that one. Trust me. I don't think they're going to check about high school anymore. It's all about the now. Ease? Is that your real name?"

"Yes," I reply matter-of-factly.

"Is that because you're easy or because you go with the flow?" I start to answer her, but she interrupts saying, "Come on, let me help you up."

As Leah offers her hand, I think that I don't need any help but reluctantly grab her hand anyway. In the next instant, a bolt of electricity shoots out through our hands. Boom! Immediately we let go and I fall back to the floor again!

World-Side: Out of body Starmark...

Shaking my hand I declare, "Wow, you shocked me! What's up with that?"

Leah at the same time looks at her hand and says, "Hmm. I am a bit shocking to some souls, but this is new." Leah looks to see that I'm still in shock but offers her hand again. Cautiously, I move to take it. This time, I feel a distinct tingling as I finally get to my feet. I hold her hand a moment longer as the tingling continues to grow. Suddenly I'm aware that she's aware of my lingering touch as I scramble to change the focus and release her hand.

Sensing my awkwardness, Leah says, "It's time to get you out of here and go explore!"

"What about Roy?"

Leah looks around the room and says, "Time is

short. It's all about us right now!" She takes my hand firmly now and looks me square in my eyes saying, "Come on Ease, it's time to get your life jumpstarted and I'm just the woman to do it!" As she leads me out the door and down the hall, I know somehow this is a beginning, but of what I'm not sure.

CHAPTER FOUR

"The first and most important truth is that we are choice!"

World-Side: Remembering my first healing

As I sit in class, I'm unable to focus. The subject is boring and so is the grad assistant that's attempting to teach it! Instead, I find myself drawn to the cloudy day and drift back to a distant memory. Wow, what a great day to be five! I get to play all day! I run out the front door and into the front lawn. I reach my arms up to the sky and begin to spin around. I go around and around and around some more until gravity and a laugh bring me down to the ground. There's Dad mowing the lawn. There's Mom planting flowers. I wonder where my brother Joe is. It doesn't matter. I'm going to be a pilot today. I've got a lot of flying to do.

I carefully inspect my cardboard plane and how it has held up since the last rain. The wings are a bit wilted, but she'll still fly. I slowly enter the cabin and prepare for takeoff. A last check of my instruments and we're flying! Wow. Bank to the left, bank to the right and we're all clear!

Suddenly, I feel fear and pain coming from my gut. Something is very wrong. I don't feel right. I was fine just a second ago but now it's all wrong! Looking up and around, I notice Dad sitting on the ground. I wonder what he's doing. Let's go see. The great thing about magic planes is that you don't have to land them. You just get out. I still feel funny in my gut as I run to where Dad is sitting.

As I approach, I see that he's crying and holding his foot! This is wrong! Dad never cries! Through his tears he looks up at me and yells, "Turn off the mower and go get your mother!" Wow! Dad only let me turn off the mower one time before. So, I guess I don't know what's going on. Mowers are loud things and they're a little scary, but I've just got to do it. So, I move over to where the switch is and push the button. It takes a few seconds but finally the mower is quiet. The sound of Dad crying now fills my head as I run as fast as I can to Mom's side.

Once there, the only thing I can think to say is that Dad is crying. And with that, a series of events begins to unfold around energy and healing work in my life. It becomes apparent that Dad, who is always in a hurry, slipped on the wet grass. His foot went under the mower. The mower, in turn, cut clean through his steel-toed work boot and three toes in the process.

Moments later, Mom and I help Dad to the back seat of the car. Mom tells me to get some newspaper from the house for the car floor. I didn't really understand why but now know it was because he was bleeding so much.

Mom runs inside the house and yells from the phone, "Find the end of Daddy's boot!"

I run as fast as I can to the place where he was mowing and sure enough, there it is. I grab it up and run back to the car. Time seems to slow down as I approach the car and my hands begin to tingle. I'm not afraid or scared at all as I look at the toes still in the end of Dad's boot. They seem to be more like building blocks than body parts. Once I get back to the car, I see Dad is still bleeding a lot and the floor of the back seat is now a puddle of bloody newsprint. I can't seem to take my eyes off his foot. All I want to do is touch it! My hands feel so hot and tingly like I'm holding a cup of hot chocolate on a cold winter's day. A moment later, I get pushed aside and watch as Mom quickly drives away.

Grandma came over in the next few minutes with the fear of God in her eyes. She always finds something to worry about. So, this will be fuel for the next three months for sure!

The bell rings marking the end of class as I collect my books and head to my next class. That event was such a long time ago. I wonder why that came up. In hindsight, it was that day, that event, that moment when I first noticed my healing gift. My hands tingle just thinking about it. Through a child's eyes, all I wanted to do is put Daddy's toes back on and heal him so that he would stop crying. The irony here is that I had, in that moment, all the faith, love and light in my being to do just that! To heal! Souls are funny about events like that one.

For Dad, it was always about being present, or not present, as the case may be. To that end, years later while mowing the lawn, you guessed it! He chose to cut off his boot again! The funniest part of it is that his toes were not there to cut off this time. As Spirits, we sure can create profound moments to bring ourselves to the present! Dad, however, never did get to a place of being present in his lifetime. But hey, that's why we have more than one lifetime to get it right!

World-Side: College courses to choose

After a couple of quarters under my belt, I've realized that college isn't what I expected it to be. As I look through the course catalog, I want to take everything! I could be here a hundred years and still want more. It's funny though that no matter what class I go to, the professors act as though they are teaching the most important information on campus. It feels like a competition instead of a complementary union of intention. It just seems like a lot of posturing and self-importance to me. Who knew that this would be a precursor to life in the world?

Ok! I need to focus a bit more on my current task.

I have courses to choose. Let's see. Yes, a class on flying. Now we're talking. Yes, a bit of calculus, a bit of science and something expressive. How about a theater class? Maybe I'll try acting for non-majors.

Just then there's a knock at my door. But of course! Leah has come in the nick of time to save me from my planning mode and get me back into the middle of being! Leah has become the star of our freshmen class. She gets invited to all the events, both social and sporting, and somehow still manages to keep up her grades. It is truly amazing to watch Leah work a crowd. I have a feeling that she will never actually have to buy anything during this lifetime. We all just seem to get swept away in her field of passion.

Pre-Life: Reflection pool: our harmonic moment

The upcoming incarnation is starting to take shape literally as I ponder my World-Side shell. I've explored so many form combinations over the centuries, yet I continue to resonate with the one I sport now. I study my own reflection looking back at me within the reflection pool. I do, however, have a few more contracts to refine and integrate before selecting my final shell design. I find it so very perfect with the science of attraction that our shell choice effortlessly allows our lessons, choices, and understanding to come to us. Like the moth to the flame, we are a beacon to all we choose to experience. In that moment, Jade moves in slowly beside me as to align our reflections side by side. Her smile inspires mine as our auras begin to change and mingle.

"Hello, Voyor. I'm so happy to see you or should I say reflect you. Are you reflecting or reflecting?"

"Both, Jade. And what brings you here?"

"You of course, my funny friend."

Shaking my head, "I'm in for trouble today. I can just feel it!"

Smiling back with almost blinding radiance Jade answers, "How about bliss instead?"

We both stand up to face each other as we have many times before. Slowly, purposely, we move our hands so that there is but a moment of space between her fingertips and mine. Then, as with so many times before, we begin to search toward each other's souls.

Joyfully, effortlessly, and lovingly our energies flow and pulse to the rhythm of music not heard but felt. In one moment, I feel her passion roll through me like the tide meets the shore. In the next moment, my being expands to touch the edges of her soul. And so, it is!

As I float in her waves, I remember Lor had commented about watching us on occasion. Lor said that we seem to transcend time and space each time we come to this place no matter where Mara is! Mara also experiences an inner glow of knowing when we are sharing. It seems that the three of us are now linked in a web of being beyond our collective understanding. We have created a magic that beckons us.

Finally, I pull my being back to the edge of my

shell space. Jade, feeling my movement does the same as we disengage and conclude our harmonic moment. Quietly, we continue to smile for a while longer. Eventually, Jade breaks the silence with, "Voyor, have you given additional thought to the intent of our contract?"

In my mind, I wonder sometimes why we use words to communicate at all. I know it's practice for World-Side but here and now, they do not serve me! I knew why Jade sought me out long before she approached the reflection pool. I begin with, "Dearest Jade, I wish I knew! I feel so torn, so divided, so lost when it comes to us. I never expected to feel this way. I am so moved by us that my body aches for you, yet I am still within my being."

With the tenderest of touches, Jade places her hand on my shoulder and whispers, "It's okay, my dear Voyor. It is Mara that fills your void. Does she not?"

"You know me so well. So well indeed. I inquired with the Senior about your path. You are so very focused and bold indeed. But why do you speak of Mara?"

Jade puts her finger to my lips and shares, "Because I know. I know that you are the only soul in the history of being that has not explored the oneness of another on World-Side. Unlike all before you, you hold a vision, a vision of a perfect union for all your being. You have quietly watched the bliss of your soul pod members through countless lifetimes. Yet, you harbor no malice, envy, or desire. How can that be? You are like a master of a topic you have yet to explore."

I sit down on one of the benches by the pool and motion for Jade to do the same. I begin with, "You deserve to know my path. Early in my journey, I explored a notion of what is effective or not. At first, I thought it only to be a manifestation of ego but after a few more lifetimes, I felt it had merit. After speaking to the Guiding Console, I requested a perspective and understanding that embraced the very essence of efficiency. I was taken to a special chamber to view a ninth-dimension demonstration model of the Yin/Yang symbol. It was so beautiful and clear. I could walk through it. Fly around it. I could even feel it. I became it! I continued to explore this space for many cycles and finally came to an understanding of principles that usually comes to a soul on the back side of their journey. I now possess an understanding that one need only actively embrace half of the working experiences of beingness to allow for completion."

Jade looks at me with a blank expression saying, "How could one ever find understanding with only half the experiences?"

"Okay, in the beginning of beingness, from our perspective, there was a moment in our wholeness when we wondered. In the next moment, we divided into a measure of perspectives called souls. Hence, you and I at that moment came into ourselves as part of the one. Next, each one of us was charged both figuratively and literally with the intention to radiate out and away from source using up our energy as we went. Farther, farther, still farther we traveled into the void of our own experience until we no longer had any energy remaining."

"With energy gone, we are adrift. We float within the sea of space and time itself. Our journey away, and how we got to that moment, is now recorded, and safely stored in our memories. This is, in many ways, a reflection of the time we now spend in Pre-Life. Here, we prepare, plan, and impassion our intentions to continue our expansion before we go to World-Side. We are on this side of conception and the gleam in our parents' eyes."

"In the next moment, we've come into a physical world of choice. Now, let's return our focus back to our spirit journey. Again, with energy to travel away from source gone, our soul turns to face source, our origin, and our home. We are in a state of choice and will. We no longer have the energy to go farther away but instead are filled with the knowing to return."

"Three truths now appear within us. The first and most important truth is that we are choice! We are empowered to navigate back to source on any path we choose. The only wrong choice is simply not to choose! The second truth is that we will interact with other souls along the way. The result of this interaction, as measured by direction, speed and intention, always results in an equal and opposite reaction of energy. Finally, we will conclude our journey by sharing the results with source as a whole."

"Now, let's look at our present moment. You've been World-Side how many times now?"

"Nine hundred and forty-two times. How many for you?"

"Me, I'm at fourteen hundred and forty. Ok, that indicates that you and I are on the home stretch so to speak regarding ascension. A few more laps and we'll be done. Yay, for us!" We both smile with the anticipation of being complete again.

"Like all beings, each of us chooses to start at a different time so we are all staggered on our way back. As we near the origin, we gain momentum and focus. We can see each other more clearly with each passing moment, still we are not yet whole. The beauty and magic are now in the sharing! We near the origin and each other. In these next moments we can choose to share our truth, our journey, and our knowingness. By doing so, we have the opportunity to experience each other's journeys without having to travel them!"

Jade raises her hand for me to pause and I do. I see her process all that I have said with the concern of finding a false notion of truth. Suddenly she smiles with a newfound joy, a knowing and a bliss that begins to reinvent her!

Looking at me with a newfound calm, she says, "Please continue."

"With this level of understanding, I pose to you the following possibility. I have longed to find my knowing in the most elegant of ways, a way that flows effortlessly and requires little or no focus. This is the magical possibility of pure being. It is this journey that I have chosen to explore. For my part, I have focused on exploring a very specific half of knowingness. At the same time, the rest of my soul pod has made every effort to explore the complementary opposite half of knowingness. In this way, we are Yin and Yang to each other."

"So, you had or have no redundant exploration in your group?"

I nod and say, "Very little," seeing that Jade's understanding grows more quickly now.

"But how did you do that? That seems almost impossible!"

"You're right. This is rare air indeed. We had to establish and invest in a foundation of truth first and foremost before going forward. And no one in our group owns that more than Lorna. She is the standard bearer of our truth!"

"In so many lifetimes the compassion and love of each other tempted each of us to edit our truth. For the most part however, we have been true to each other. On World-Side we call that tough love!"

Jade wonders aloud, "So you're saying that the entire group is unique in their personal exploration?"

"Actually, no. Only two of the group remains a clear complement to me: you and Mara."

As if witnessing her first sunrise, Jade exclaims, "So this is why our blending is different than with all others I experience?"

Resolvedly I say, "For us, the more unique our knowingness is, the stronger our attraction becomes. The world saying, 'opposites attract' has never been truer!"

"What about the others in the group?"

Reflecting for a moment, I share, "A lot can happen in a thousand lifetimes. Most often one of the supporting souls in each of our soul pods would find themselves at an impasse. This is a karmic clog so to speak. This is a phase when they incarnate several times with no success regarding their intentions. It was in these times most always that one of the souls in my group sacrificed our shared intention to help one in their soul pod."

Jade shakes her head in disbelief, "So you're saying that somehow, some way, with no known intention, I have found my way to you! How can that be?"

Looking gently into Jade's eyes I reply, "You are my miracle, and I am yours!"

Jade's excitement turns to concern, "But what of Mara. How does she fit into this? I still don't understand. She has been at your side from eternity. She has been mirroring your every choice. She has complemented your being in every way and given sway to your choices over hers. How do you know which of us to choose?"

As I hear the question fill the air between her lips and my ears, I feel quite blank and surrender, "I don't know…"

CHAPTER FIVE

"I've chosen to be 'born with a veil'!"

World-Side: Ease is 23 and a junior in college

PEERING INTO THE mirror, I see a strapping fellow of twenty-three looking back. I see a young man that finds himself in the middle of his junior year of college. No more am I the wise fool of yesteryear, nor am I the master of anything. I need to hurry a bit if I have any hope of catching up with Leah tonight. Man, that girl can party! Looking back on the last three years, you'd think we would have taken at least one class together but it's always the same, at the last second one of us always drops or changes. What's that about?! I mean really, I've wanted to kiss her. Take her in my arms and hold her next to me. It just never seems like the right moment. I always feel her. I'm sure she's got to feel me too! Looking back into the mirror and speaking to my reflection I say, "Ok big guy, it's time to rock!"

World-Side: Going uptown

As the colorful tapestry of fall surrenders to the first chill of winter, I observe an endless stream of brave souls making their weekly migration uptown. The place is an enigma unto itself by supporting fifty-two bars within a three-block area. Here, each of us focus on getting away from the grind of learning. It seems crowded already, even for an early Friday night.

I'm supposed to catch up with Leah at Swanky's but that never seems to happen. I'm utterly hopeful tonight since Leah finally broke up with Jimmy. Before her, I've never seen a girl have boyfriend after boyfriend since the second day of school. It's like there's an invisible queue or something. Each new guy starts up with her in hopes of warming himself in her glow, only to become the fuel for it. In the end it's always the same as she allows them to understand that they will never meet her needs. Of course, I'm on the other end of the story. I seem to be the perfect friend who's the boy, but not the boyfriend! No matter, I'm worth the wait!

The music blares in the half-lit bar and the stench of cheap beer fills the air. It's sure hard to see in here but that looks like Manson over there with the guys. I walk over yelling, "Hey Manson!"

Manson looks up with a smile and high-fives me saying, "Hey Ease, pull up a chair. How's things?"

I couldn't help but flash back to that victory over my fear and how Manson and I have since become the best of friends. It's so ironic that the very guy I feared has ultimately helped me find my own power several times growing up. And at the end, every time he simply said, "Hey dude, I got your back." In the quietest of moments, you can feel the love. A beer bottle suddenly wizzes past my head and I note that this, however, is not one of those times!

After I've settled in and had a few beers, Leah makes her grand entrance with a guy on each arm. She is obviously feeling no pain as she stumbles to the dance floor. I find it frustrating to see the men that Leah chooses. Most of the time, they're captains of this sport or that, but rarely anything to write home about. I've been meaning, as a friend, to ask her about that but I'm still not sure if it's any of my business.

But back to Leah! When I watch her dance, every part of her body seems to move and flow with the music. It doesn't matter what kind of music is playing. She's just a joy to behold.

Most of the time, Leah is very much in control of herself, her date, and her surroundings but tonight is an exception. The song ends and Leah spots me. She is two sheets to the wind as she struggles to walk. It's time to be a friend so I stand and gently say, "Leah, what's up? We were supposed to get together an hour ago."

She moves up to me and places both her arms over my shoulders. Staring into my eyes for a moment she says, "Jimmy is an ass. I'm so over him! You want to be my boyfriend?"

I'm speechless and a bit concerned as I focus to hold her up.

She continues, "You know you want me. You know I want you. I should have jumped you that first day on the floor. But no! I thought Roy was my soulmate. What the hell did I know?! Come on big boy take me. Take me now!"

At this point, Manson and the guys are out of control as they start razzing me, "Hey, if you don't take Leah, I will."

I need to do something fast. "Ok Leah, let's get out of here."

Leah smiles, "It's about time. Your place or mine?"

"Your place is closer."

Leah tries to kiss me countless times on the way back to her place, while I'm focused on the task of not dropping her. What ill fate is this that finds me having to resist the very thing my heart yearns to explore?

Finally, I get her to her house and bed. She looks up at me for a moment with thankful eyes and then falls fast asleep. I wonder, in times like these, how Leah's life is going to unfold. She is, in this moment, so very peaceful. As I look at her, a part of her seems destined for greater things if she could just find something to be passionate about. Before I leave her room, I find a piece of paper and write, "You're all right!" Pausing for a moment, I add, "I'm all right too. Ease."

The next day, I see Leah in line at the bookstore. "Hey Leah, how are you feeling?"

She grabs her head, "You don't want to know."

"You got all your books for next semester?"

"No. Are you taking chemistry?"

I shake my head, "No that stuff just doesn't rock my world. Are you?"

She looks over her sunglasses with a gleam in her eye as she adds, "I don't know, it might be fun as long as you're not taking it!" We both laugh. She adds, "We're still batting a thousand. No common classes! Speaking of taking it, did you see me last night?"

Realizing she hadn't seen the note, I reply, "You, no I didn't see you at all."

"Funny, I had the weirdest dream about us. It seemed so real."

Feeling a bit odd, I added, "I'll catch up later," and left to be by myself.

Pre-Life: Meeting Kara for a simulator session

On my way to our session in the Holo-Matrix, I run into Kara. She appears to be especially emotional by the look of her aura. It seems like she's a hundred shades of orange as she says, "Hey Voyor, walking my way?"

"Wouldn't miss it."

The Holo-Matrix is a simulator that assists us in experiencing what it will be like to express certain gifts on World-Side before they are available to our shells. The easiest example is playing a piano at the age of three. In this example, the soul must understand and practice playing with the body and, specifically, with the hand size of a three-year-old.

If I were to phase into the shell form for a moment,

I would wiggle my fingers and feet and realize that I can't reach the keys or pedals and there's no custom piano anywhere in sight. But I'm not here to play the piano today. For me, it's more about increasing my mental focus in planning to select visionary sight as one of my skill sets in the coming incarnation. I believe this skill, more than anything else I select, will serve me both in the long term and possibly as an income source.

Kara has also selected visionary sight as a skill set but for a different reason. For her, vision will allow her to be a seer on World-Side with the ability to look through the veil as a psychic. The most amusing aspect for both of us is simply looking through the veil. In all cases, the sum of knowingness is always available to use all the time if we just embrace a focused intention. We all are psychic on World-Side but rarely realize it and utilize the gift. The trick is not to be distracted by the reflections from World-Side. It's like the sky is really a pool of water when we, as humans, look for answers and insight. We often mistake our own reflections as the information we're looking for. Conversely, world history notes many of its most profound discoveries as being channeled simultaneously to different souls. Time after time, great inventors looked up into the heavens to see the same vision at the same time. I love the symbolism. This vision will also serve as one of the clues we can leave as a thread to our mission.

So, to bring attention and focus to my seeing gift, I chose to be 'born with a veil'! This veil, referred to as a caul, is a piece of the amniotic sac still attached to a newly born baby's head or face, and is easily removed. Quite rare, it only occurs in one out of eighty thousand births and is believed to be an omen of psychic ability and vision. Legends say that ship captains, during the sixteenth and seventeenth centuries, paid upwards of the equivalent of three hundred dollars for one of these cauls and then hung it on the bow of their ship. It was said that the magic allowed the captain to see through the fog of unseen waters.

Kara and I wait for two simulators. Because we are from the same soul pod, we will practice together. In this way, we create an additional opportunity to interact on World-Side. It's like the gift of being born a healer. I am thrilled at the notion of working with some of the very best healers in the coming time, provided of course that we can transcend our own self-imposed limitations. It never matters what paths we've taken to use our skills, but simply that we are there in the moment and that we are in the now of our beingness! That's why we choose ascension!

I look up to see the staging light turn to green and say to Kara, "It's our moment." Kara and I enter adjacent chairs in front of a Holo-Screen. We start by seeing a common object and an intention of what that object will look like or evolve to in a span of three World-Side years. I've invested much effort in this skill set so I normally evolve two or three versions of the object, based on the additional parameters of a World-Side notion of cost and usage. Once I realize these versions in my mind, I select one and mentally send it to Kara. I don't really send it to her as much as I simply broadcast from my mind. She in turn, scans my being for any formation of energy and uses it to create a mental snapshot of my vision. The differences being that her vision is static, for the most part, and my vision is dynamic to the extent that I also understand how and why the object works.

We cascade effortlessly through a hundred objects during our session. Each object in the sequence grows more complex. At times however, Kara cannot help but giggle at the images she scans from my mind. This is primarily because there are moments when all I can think about is Mara!

World-Side: "It's a surprise!"

I have been thinking about Leah every day since the bar incident. I can't seem to shake how she dates who she dates. So, to honor myself and maybe a good friend, I've planned a picnic. The campus is so beautiful in the spring, and I have the perfect place to go. It's quiet with a stream, a big shade tree, and me. Of course, it doesn't hurt to include a great bottle of wine, a loaf of fresh bread, and some cheeses that complete the trio.

Leah is in a special mood today. Her voice sounds somewhat eager and reflective on the phone.

"Are you ready? I'm out in front," I say.

"Do I need to bring anything?"

"Just yourself!"

As an excited Leah exits the front door of her apartment, she looks at me with joyful eyes. Still speaking into her phone, she yells, "I'm here!"

We both yell, "Yeah! Road trip!"

Looking around for any clues, Lea asks, "Where are we going?"

"It's a surprise!"

She gets into the car, full of anticipation, yet calm in a knowing way. The breeze dances in her golden hair, paired with the reflection of the sun. It doesn't take long to drive to the parking area. Once there, I grab the picnic basket out of the trunk.

Upon seeing it, Leah says, "A picnic, why didn't you tell me? I could have brought something."

In general, Leah can't stand surprises, so she tries to see what's in the basket. I gently push her hand away saying, "It's a surprise! You're just going to have to wait and receive!"

Leah stops for a moment and asks, "Receive?"

"Yes receive. For me, today is all about giving. Pure giving! So let me give! It's so funny to me that we are all give-aholics to some degree. The sad part is that we're not really giving at all. Let's walk and talk."

I grabbed the blanket, the basket and started down a little-used path.

World-Side: The act of giving and receiving

I start with asking Leah, "Ok Leah, if I made you a five-course meal with all the trimmings, how many seconds would go by until you were thinking of what to give back?"

Leah smiles, "Two seconds. Why?"

"This is my point. You, in that moment, haven't even allowed yourself to receive. We don't take a moment to be present with our gift. Instead, our mind is already in giving mode."

A bit defensive, Leah says, "So what! That's just what friends do!"

Shaking my head, I say "No, no, no! By thinking of giving during the act of receiving you do neither! You're just playing the exchange game!"

Leah's energy turns to curiosity, "Go on."

"Society has conditioned us to think that if we don't reciprocate a giving gesture, then somehow that makes us unfeeling, uncaring, or selfish! But what's really happening? The fact is that we aren't doing either. We're simply consuming under the guise of love. Let's jump back in time to when I picked you up. Here I am, full of joy for the effort and intention I've invested to honor you. So, anything more than allowing you to acknowledge my efforts would take away from your receiving and in the end cancel out my gift. So, if you feel the need to give back, allow that process to be separated with a moment of you loving and allowing yourself to be loved!"

Leah grabs me from behind and spins me around, "Aww!" Her eyes are full of passion as she hugs me deeply for a long moment.

I struggle to receive her energy and not drop the basket. This hug is different somehow. It's more real. Nothing else seems to be present in the world except us! I can't help but say, "It's like we're pure energy!"

"Maybe we are!"

Leah releases me as she lets out a big laugh. Like dancing on a cloud, Leah skips ahead on the path and then returns to me. Each time she skips back she smiles and says, "Are we there yet?" Seemingly she went back and forth twenty times before we walked into the clearing and within the gentle sound of a small waterfall.

Leah stops in the moment and stares. In her silence, Leah has a glow about her. Tears slowly drift down her face as a feeling of joy overwhelms her. Allowing her to savor the moment, I go to a grassy spot and spread the blanket. I, like Leah, am in a state of edgeless joy! It's peace of beingness that requires no words, no deeds, and no cares!

Leah slowly comes back to the present and is delighted to see a perfect little picnic spread. Against a lush spot of green grass, a plaid blanket frames a chilling bottle of wine. The freshly cut bread warmed and boasting of the energy I projected into it a moment before. The cheese is sliced and arranged on a silver tray. All are accented by the scent of three lavender candles.

Leah is still until I motion her to join me. She kicks off her shoes to feel the grass beneath her feet and slowly moves to a rhythm all her own.

I watch her feel each breath as she nears. In this moment, I'm filled with anticipation, excitement, and passion! Although my intention was to give and support, I am filled with a raging desire to hold her. Take her! Be one with her! She has become my sight, my air, my all. I dare not move for I might break the spell that binds us.

Suddenly we hear two hawks cry out as they swoop by us. They circle us from above as we watch from below. Each of us curious of the other's point of view. They seem to be calling out to us and each other. The hawks have come as omens and messengers. They are messages to be present of knowing and choice.

We look at each other and smile. Leah sits down on the blanket as I pour her a glass of wine. She takes it and studies my facial expression. I say, "What?"

"I don't know. You just seem different somehow. I'm not really sure what's different but you don't look the same."

All I can do is smile in agreement as I feel Leah's eyes pass through my shell and into my soul.

We speak about many topics this perfect spring day, but no words are about us. I did come to ask about her choices of men and am totally surprised as she shares, "Ease, I just don't want to be part of their stuff. Relationships are part of my day, not the center of my life! The less we talk the easier it is to save myself from me."

Leah can say more with a silent gaze than speaking all the words in the world. But she continues, "I have my challenges this time around. But for the most part, I just get bored. I feel like I'm going to explode with all this passion! So, I find a dense hunk of a guy and rock."

As I watch Leah speak, I can't help but notice that we are changed forever. I always saw Leah as a party girl, yet somehow my heart has just skipped a beat. I'm moved to say, "Dear one, you just need another outlet to vent all that passion. What's been your favorite class so far?"

Leah thinks long and hard and finally shares, "Good question. I guess interior design was okay, but the weird thing is I sort of love the chemistry class I took last semester. I got a B and never did any homework. I just got it! It's sort of like a plan and a mystery with attitude."

"So why not choose that as a major?"

Leah rolls her eyes, "My dad would kill me. I'm already a junior and I only took the intro as a core requirement. I don't think he's up for the five-year plan!"

"So, what! If I were your dad and you came home for break excited about your passion for a hard science, I'd be thrilled."

I can tell that Leah is not quite getting my point. "Remember Leah, your dad wants his little girl to make a living to get you out of the house. Unless of course, college is the only way you're going to find a husband."

I knew that would get her fired up. Leah's eyes become large and fiery as she hits me hard in the arm. We both laugh as she adds, "Point taken!"

The afternoon soon turns into early dusk as the sun shines low in the sky. We laugh and drink as the clouds slowly move by. Many times, we almost kiss, yet for some unknown reason we both choose to resist…

CHAPTER SIX

"I sure do like little miracles!"

Pre-Life: Light falls: So many shells, so little time…

WITH THE SUNSET forming a rainbow sky, I see Lorna walking up the path to the falls. Her radiant glow reflects a thoughtful look as I slowly move to join her. She stops, turns to face me, and raises her hands to experience me. We blend for a long moment until she speaks, "Voyor, I'm feeling so unsure about my soul pod contracts. I only have a few cycles left and I haven't even selected my parents or brother yet."

To comfort her I say, "It's all perfect Lorna. You're doing well. What's your prime intention this time?"

"The usual. I choose to master truth."

I shake my head and add, "Oh, that's a challenging one. Who is your primary mirror?"

"That's just it; I'm going in circles on this. One minute, I feel like the parent and child roles will serve me but then I become concerned that I won't get a clean closure to it."

I wrap my arms around her and ask, "Okay, back to basics. Which gender have you chosen to be?"

Lorna pulls out a small device about the size of a cell phone and turns it on. A voice asks, "Male or female version?" Lorna says, "Female." The device projects a holo-image that slowly rotates for us.

I'm amazed at the detail Lorna has invested in the shell design. I comment, "Wow, effective form. Let's see the male version." The device changes the holo-image to the male version. "What gender do you want to be this time?" I ask.

"I'm leaning heavily towards being female. I have been a male my last three incarnations. Why do you ask?"

Taking a deep breath, I offer, "This is what I hear you saying. You are a bit frustrated with the male form's potential, yet you're also concerned about the emotional web regarding a parent and child contract. Have you worked all the combinations within your group?"

"Yes," she says hesitantly.

Wondering, I say, "You don't seem to be so sure."

Lorna sighs, "Some of these combinations were so long ago."

In agreement I add, "I hear you! May I suggest an approach to take?"

"Yes, please do."

I continue, "Ok, clear your head. Visualize which

relationship you feel has the most potential of emotional webbing?"

"That's easy, the mother and daughter combination."

"And what side is more tainted to the truth?"

"The mother."

"Why is that?"

"Social conditioning of the current age."

"Ok, which relationship is the most even?"

Lorna thinks a moment and says, "Brother and brother."

"Why so?"

"Well, once they get through the 'I'm first and you're younger' stuff, they just don't seem to care. On the other hand, a sister-to-sister bond is like the tide. One moment they are as close as they can be and the next it can be crushing. The process is endless."

Feeling that we're making progress, I move forward, "Great, now what's your primary intention again?"

Lorna firmly states, "Mastery of truth!"

"Ok, so if you choose to be the elder brother and transcend the ego of that role quickly by endowing the younger brother to have an exceptional gift and the mother and father don't express their emotions, then what are you left with?"

Lorna takes a big deep breath and exclaims, "A high probability platform for the exploration of truth!"

We smile, knowing that life is about probabilities not certainties, but that's the trick. Excited I add, "Lorna, if you add that contract into your shell form design, and add the condition of family wealth, what do you get?"

Lorna plugs in the new criteria. The unit replies, "Update complete." We both look with pleasure at the refined form. I ask Lorna, "How do you feel about this shell's ability to support your mastery now?"

She giggles, "Bravo!" She hugs me and adds, "You're so good at shell design. How do you know?"

"It's just the place I am on the wheel. Remember, the trick is not to confuse the roles we play with the soul we are!"

"How does this work with your contract with Mara?" she asks.

"This will help bring us to the conclusion we have both explored for many lifetimes. Do you have a name for the revised shell?"

Lorna looks at the image and then at me saying, "I think I'll choose Marshal."

World-Side: Ease's senior year at college

Wow, senior year! This year is nothing but research, friends, and fun! Hmm, I think I'm going to wear long sleeves for the game today. Those guys from South Quad can get a little rough!

Manson walks through the doorway, ready to rock and saying, "Go red, baby!"

We exchange high-fives up and down as he asks, "You ready, Ease?"

"Yes Manson. It's time for a little revenge. South

beat us badly, in the beginning of the season, when we didn't have you. But this time will be different. As my protection, I always have time to find an open guy to throw to. You rock!"

As games of touch football go, I'll never really understand why we call it touch. Normally, the ball carrier always gets brutally tackled and then the defense grabs their flag and throws it down at him. Boys will be boys, I guess.

As Manson and I walk to the field, we can smell football in the air. It must be something about the late cut grass of autumn and the slight chill in the air that inspires the need to play.

So far, it's been a good game for Manson. He, as usual, has everyone in fear and I've already thrown for three scores. It looks like it will come down to this last defensive stand. If we hold them, we'll win. Normally Manson just plays offense but hey, it's the end of the game and the season. As he rushes the passer, another blocker hits Manson near his eye with a ring. Everything stops as Manson grabs his eye and yells, "No jewelry, you ass!" As Manson kneels in pain, the other team concedes the game. Winning in this moment feels very hollow as Manson reveals a large gash above his left eye.

World-Side: A little miracle with Manson's eye

Both teams say their farewells, but my attention is centered on Manson. We're on our way back to my room as Manson swears, "Damn it! The last frigging' play of the last game and I get nicked! Lorrie is going to kill me. We're supposed to go out tonight and meet her parents. Shit, shit, shit!"

In a calming manner I offer, "Hey big guy, no worries. Let's get some ice on it and I'll take a look."

"Thanks Ease, but I'll need more than first aid on this. That ass got me good."

"Ok, how important is tonight for you?"

"You have no idea!"

Suddenly a distant memory returns to me as I smile and offer, "Ok, how about a little miracle?"

"'Little miracle,' what are you talking about?"

With comfort I add, "Look you've got nothing to lose and everything to gain, so hear me out. Remember that necklace made of copper with the red gem I've been wearing?"

Manson, holding his head, says, "Yes. How could I not? You've been wearing that thing for months."

"Exactly! Up to now, I've been charging it up. I just didn't know what for."

"I don't follow."

"Ok, think about when you cut a finger. You look at it and say to yourself, 'darn that cut will take a few weeks to heal' right?"

Not understanding this, Manson replies, "Right. So what?"

"So, it heals. It heals all by itself. The cells know what to do. But, if you put an antibiotic on it, then you expect it to heal faster. The cream works to speed up the process by allowing the cells to focus on healing and not fighting an infection. Right?"

"Right. I get it. Healing 101. So where are you going with this?"

Excited, I share, "If we place an energy field around the wound and suspend your notion of how long it will take to heal, then it will heal faster. You've seen it for yourself. Remember when our running back broke his leg in the second game of the season and the doc used that light electrode charge machine on him?"

"Yes."

"So, what happened?"

Manson's eyes grow a bit bigger as he says, "He got back on the field in a month!"

Excited, I respond, "Exactly! The break healed thirty percent faster!"

Manson still in pain says, "Yes, but I didn't break my leg and we don't have a month."

Thoughtfully I add, "Ok big guy, home stretch. If you can believe that your cut can heal in an hour than it can! I'll do all the work. You just need to believe!"

Manson starts to speak but I stop him with, "No buts! No try! Do or don't do!"

We both laugh and say, "Yoda!" in unison.

Moments later, we're in my room and I ask Manson to lie down on the bed. I put some ice on his forehead to redirect his focus and retrieve the medallion from the nightstand. As I examine the gash I think, "This is so perfect. I've got the perfect tool. The copper will serve as a conductor and the red ruby will supply additional energy." I place the medallion gently on Manson's gash and hold my hands over and above his head. I don't really understand what I'm doing at this point, but it feels right.

I say, "Relax Manson, just take three deep breaths in and out."

Manson has now moved to a very relaxed place as I turn my attention to the gash.

I can see the gash in my head like it's under a magnifying glass. It looks like an eye shape of cells. Wow, the cells are like little balls. Some in the middle are broken but near the edge they look good; there're just simply separated. Something inside me says start at the edges and direct the cells to come together like magnets attract. Nothing seems to happen until the edges begin to bond closed! Once a few of the edge cells come together, I notice some extra stuff, from the broken cells, I guess. My inner voice says, "Move your hands close and then away." As I do so, the extra stuff seems to soak into the gash and disappear. Wow, this rocks!!!

It now seems like the time to include Manson in the process. I begin by saying, "Manson visualize the gash as a little tear in your coat. Not big, not deep, just a clean little tear. Okay, now from the end of the tear, I want you to see some thread made of light. We're going to move that thread through one side of the tear and out the other side. Next, we'll gently pull it closed. Rock on! Great job! Ok, again, start with the edge of one side, through the other and pull it closed."

This goes on for about twenty more minutes until my inner voice says, "You're done. Let Manson rest for five more minutes and then have him drink some water."

Doing as I was told; I help Manson up after I take the medallion off his head. To my amazement and delight, the gash is practically gone! What is left is no more than a small cut. No bruises, no blood, nothing but a small cut. Manson looks really woozy right now as I hand him some water. He feels where the gash was and asks, "How's it looking?"

In that moment, I realize that I hadn't let him see the gash at all. Regarding this healing, ignorance is bliss. I reply to Manson, "You handsome devil, you're going to look great tonight!"

Manson feels the area some more and declares, "Wow, it doesn't hurt at all. What did you do again?"

Thinking of the miracle I just observed, I reply, "Nothing but watch you heal yourself big guy!"

Manson stands up and looks in the mirror saying, "I'm good. No big deal. Let me see that medallion of yours." I hand it to Manson, and he looks closely at both sides saying, "Where's the ruby you mentioned? It must have fallen out."

He hands the medallion back to me and to my surprise I agree that the ruby is no longer there. Manson looks at his watch and moves to leave. Thoughtfully, he stops and turns in the doorway saying, "Wow Ease, I don't know what you do, but I sure do like 'little miracles'!"

World-Side: Not bad for winging it

Well, its seven weeks until graduation and I still haven't declared a major. Being an undergrad has been fun but choosing anything to focus on seems counterproductive. To date, I managed to make the Dean's List in every college in the university, but for what? I don't feel drawn to anything; I feel drawn to everything! I want to see how it all fits together. But hey, I have a plan. I'll go down to the Office of Academic Advising today and get an advisor. Next, I'll show him my thought process and mechanics of my vision. This should be fun.

I walk down the green and past the bookstore on a warm spring day. The trees are beginning to blossom as is my desire to make my way in the world. As I enter the Advising Office, I am struck by the intensity I see in many students' eyes. This is the time of year that many of us begin to reflect on choices made and honors earned. Yet, why am I so indifferent to the process? In the end, I just feel that we are all unique but at the same time no one is special. If that simple notion were embraced, the world would be a happier place.

I meet with my advisor for an hour before parting. I believe, for the most part, he was in shock that I had navigated my course through college on my own. Wow, that only took an hour and here I am with a bachelor's degree in general studies and a triple major in electronics, computer science, and multimedia design. Not bad for winging it.

I feel time has flown as my thoughts turn to Leah. A year and a half after our picnic and she's the darling of the chemistry department! She just got her fifth job offer from a chemical corporation. There's something to be said about applying one's passion to something constructive. The funny part for her is that she no longer has time for boyfriends. I guess there is just too much to discover. We've both talked about graduate school, but I still don't know how I feel about it or her. One minute we're the best of friends, and in the next I'm lost in her eyes.

Pre-Life: Senior Council

Pre-Life staging has gone well for the most part after adjusting to our newest member, Jade. Even with that change, I still find myself on the way to Senior Council again. I'm always surprised to be invited. I wonder what they'll propose today.

I cross a large intersection of various flying pods and duck into an entry portal. The indicator on my wrist points to the right. Out of nowhere, I hear my name called, "Hey Voyor, what's up?" From behind me Kara looks all aglow.

I respond, "Kara where did you come from?"

"From my vision session, of course."

"You are radiant!"

"Thanks. How about you? Back to Senior Council again?"

I nod yes.

"Wow, Voyor that's the fourth time this cycle, isn't it?"

"My fifth, but who's counting."

We both laugh as Kara adds, "They say that happens a lot before your final."

"I hope whoever they are, they're right! See you at our next session."

Kara passes as I enter the Council-Plex. The overall structure is in the shape of a pyramid. It towers above the surrounding architecture but brings a sense of symmetry and stability to the entire region. Once inside, I enter the Grand Hall and am directed to one of the many corridors. I enter the main archway and walk to the end of the corridor. I wait there for only a moment before hearing, "Greetings Voyor, please enter the pulse in sector three." I enter sector three, move to the center of the circular pattern on the floor and clear my mind.

From out of the midst of my mind comes an image of a pyramid base made of flat square stones. I see myself walking on the foundation of the stone blocks. As I study the image, each stone illuminates to reveal an aspect label. Soon, I realize that this vision is my journey! Wow, this is like walking down memory lane. I recall my very first mastery so many eons ago. Yet it seems like only a single moment has passed.

Eventually, I come to the last block on that level and then begin to rise and hover above the whole layer. A second layer then appears, and I rediscover those masteries one block at a time in the same way. This process continues until I find myself at the very top of the structure. Before me now is a capless apex. After so many lifetimes of evolution, I am in wonder of the essence that will be required to form that capstone.

I realize that this is like building a pyramid of mastery. Senior responds, "Yes Voyor, it is exactly that. It is a pyramid of your mastery! We will call upon you again soon." Whoosh!

Pre-Life: Deciding on my major and minor career

I asked Mara to meet me in the Historic Innovation Center. I love following the thread of innovations through time. As usual, she is right on our time pulse. "How may I serve you my dear Voyor? We haven't been in these hallowed halls for many cycles." I smile and respond, "So true! I am having the most challenging time deciding on my major and minor career for our final cycle. On one hand, I would like to bring some meaningful innovation into the world but I'm reluctant to follow the science path which is affected almost always by the need to solicit funding sources." Mara agrees, "I remember those struggles all too well. What alternatives are you considering?"

I respond, "There is always the wealthy approach, but I am a bit vulnerable in stopping the design process and actually bringing an innovation to the world marketplace." Mara shakes her head in agreement saying "Wow, those were the days when creation was so much simpler." I continue, "Because of that, I am leaning toward the corporate path. While it does not lend itself to major innovation that can serve the world, it does almost always yield a series of products into the marketplace. Thoughtfully, Mara replies, "Your logic seems sound." Voyor adds, "And what about you, Mara? Have you found an approach that supports the passion you wish to share? Mara smiles "Why yes, I do. I'll be a bit of an actor this time around. I'll engage the audience very directly with words of fire for all to hear. Instead of being like Zune with a one-on-one format, I'll be speaking in front of hundreds and then thousands utilizing all manner of media." Voyor shares, "Outstanding, I can hardly wait to hear it!"

CHAPTER SEVEN

"...You are strong with the gift."

World-Side: Ease at 28 working in corporate

LOOKING BACK FROM the mirror, I see a young man of twenty-eight. Working in corporate is okay, but I wish someone had the courage in this arena to make a choice, any choice! Courage, in this context, falls into two general pools of thought. First is the realm of pure research. It is here that I find the most pleasure. To be inspired to look beyond the known and theorize what can be is the foundation of growth in every way. In contrast, functional research tends to fall in the realm of profit-based intentions. It is here that our brightest minds are asked to create the maximum number of product innovations instead of releasing product versions that would best serve the public at large. Being new to working in industry, I am constantly assigned projects that require one to think outside the box or that require costly time and materials to complete. The more successful I become, the more attention I garner from what I call "the brotherhood of failure." The brotherhood consists of all the up-and-coming executives which, in their climb up the corporate ladder, are given the task of "slaying the dragon."

The dragon is the task that no one, to date, has been able to complete. Most attempts are dismissed almost immediately with the complexity and scope far beyond any young executive's ability to even comprehend it, let alone engage it! As for me, it didn't take long to conceive, test, and execute a plan that slays the dragon. Within a short time, I realize that I upset the balance of the corporate ladder and find myself transferred to the manufacturing center, upon returning from a vacation.

I don't really know how much longer I can be here. The clarity of college has been blinded by the notion that we rise only to the level of our inabilities and then reside there in failure. Good thing I have some great friends to help me get by. Speaking of friends, I get to meet a new one today!

World-Side: Ease's first meeting with Zune

Zune and I meet through Jonah. I never, in a million years, would have guessed that Jonah knows someone like her but hey, it's all magic! I guess it was about a year ago that Jonah hurt his back pulling someone from a burning car. Jonah sets the standard of trust by transcending his own fears to help others. I love that man for the integrity he brings to the world with every breath he takes.

So, with the medical community stumped on what was wrong, Jonah looked elsewhere and found Zune. Jonah told me she's a Reiki Master and that her work is so amazing. I'm looking forward to meeting her. It's Friday and I'm glad to find myself anywhere other than work. It's about six o'clock in the evening as I enter a rundown part of town.

Let's see, this is the place. As I walk in, I wonder who in here would have the name Zune. I look around the space to see a wide selection of souls. Some look rather rough while others don't seem like they belong here at all. I feel like I fall into that group. Finally, I notice a dimly lit soul sitting in the corner, facing the door. She is a woman who effortlessly commands her space and I'm drawn to her.

I go to her without any hesitation but before I can say a word, she puts her finger to her lips indicating for me not to speak. She stands, faces me, and raises her hands. I've never seen this before but somehow know to place my hands opposite hers. As I close my eyes and gently touch her fingers with mine, she slowly moves hers slightly away. The funniest thing about this is that with a small gap between our fingers, I feel her healing energy kick in! It's like flipping the on-switch. This is very cool! Another moment passes by, and I open my eyes to see Zune's smiling face.

She says, "Jonah was right about you. You are strong with the gift." She motions for me to follow her as she leads me to a back room. The room is small yet expansive in its simplicity. The walls are adorned with images of spiritual masters throughout the history of soulkind. Yet it's as if we are surrounded by no walls at all.

She points to a chair, and we sit down. In life, trust is a matter of small steps and the passing of time. I do however feel a profound sense of clear trust and energy from her. We engage in countless topics and settle into some very casual conversation. A moment later, I realize that we've just talked for the fastest three hours of my life, when she notes that she needs to leave.

I'm rather lost in the moment as Zune says, "I'm giving Jonah his last session tomorrow. You and I can meet at six o'clock next Friday. Here's my card. Wear loose clothing and drink a lot of water the day before."

What do I say to that? In a lame attempt to add to the conversation, I say, "Oh no. Jonah swears by you! How can you say tomorrow is his last session?"

Zune smiles and says, "You and I have met and therefore his task is done." She begins to walk away and then stops for a moment, turns, and says, "Don't be late, be now."

Not exactly sure what just happened, I leave the room after her and notice that everyone in the place is eyeing me. Not in a bad way but eyeing me, nonetheless. As I venture outside, I am struck by the quiet presence of a nearly full moon.

The time Zune said to meet is finally here and I'm just outside the address on her card. Again, this is not the best of neighborhoods but here I am and here I go. As I climb the stairs to the third floor, I notice my hands start to tingle. The tingling continues to get stronger as I find myself standing in front of a door cracked open. Quietly I open the door and approach Zune, like the first day we met.

Without a word, I mirror her and give in to the flow. It seems like she's scanning me, but I don't feel afraid. I don't feel any emotion at all! It's like I'm a spirit! Very neat!

The moment passes as I feel Zune pull away to now sit down on the floor. She breaks the silence by asking, "Do you have any questions?"

Funny! Nothing I've done with this woman is common or normal, yet I feel blank. I reply, "No."

"Good. Ever focus on your energy much?"

I answer, "No, only when someone around me gets hurt."

"How old were you the first time?"

Remembering Dad and his foot, I answer, "About five."

"Good! I'm going to teach you Reiki. Have you heard of that before?"

I respond, "I've heard of it but really know nothing about it."

Smiling she says, "Good, then you're doubly blessed!"

In the following weeks, she guides me through the process of intention-based healing. At the same time, we really don't speak much. I just know what she wants and do it. With each level of training, I come to know a bit more about myself. I feel as if I'm doing more to heal myself than to support the healing of others. During the weeks and months that pass, Zune invites a group of her friends to attend various sessions. For the most part, it's like a long echo. They come in and receive energy work from me, smile at Zune and leave with no words exchanged.

Then comes the day when I see my first client. In the moments before the session, I review my symbols and check the space one last time. I hear Zune answer the door in the front room and greet my first client. From what I can hear, they are old friends.

Upon entering the front room, I see a woman in her late sixties that seems full of life yet captive within a failing shell. The joints of her fingers are bound and distorted, and she is unable to stand without the aid of her cane. However, her eyes show me that she is a master of her heart as she meets my eyes with timeless love. Having been here many times before, she smiles and moves slowly to the next room. She refuses help as she positions herself on the massage table after asking me to attend to her cane. Zune enters and asks if she would like any water, which she declines. Zune smiles, saying, "Enjoy," as she closes the door behind her.

Wow. It's our time now. It's time to allow me to transcend the notion of limits and for her to allow herself to receive. I'm about to ask if she is ready to begin, when to my surprise she says, "I was born ready!"

I ask her to close her eyes and begin breathing in a thoughtful way as I position myself at her feet.

With hands open, I begin to experience her energetic flow and the extent to which she is grounded. Almost immediately, I feel an imbalance from the left side to the right. I slowly travel up the right side of her body scanning with my hands as I go. Upon reaching her head, I hang for a moment to experience a very notable change in her overall field. It's like my efforts to observe her has already changed her field before I could even formalize an intention.

I finish moving down her left side and return to her feet. At this point, I feel quite torn. My body wants to direct my hands to ebb and flow with her energetic currents but my head and training struggle to grasp an understanding of the scope of her condition. What seems like an eternity of indecision on my part is but a brief moment in this world as I work toward integrating both processes.

Suddenly, I can see with my hands a triangulated pattern streaming from her right foot to her left knee. From there the energy moves to her right hip and finally up to her left shoulder. My hands intuit what to do as I mentally continue to process the patterns that I perceive. After a moment, I finally surrender my mind to the dance that my hands are already engaged in.

Back and forth, up, and down, left, and right my hands flow. The dance slows to a final clearing of all the misguided energy that her body has shed. Her whole essence has changed, as well as her breathing. Calm becomes her. I find myself at her feet again as if I've completed a circle. This time however, I am a witness to a gentle and constant energy that enters in from the crown of her head and flows effortlessly down her form and out of her feet. In this moment, her aura becomes visible to me and reveals a vibrant gold and green color. I am aware that she is in the process of allowing her healing and that our session is complete.

Suddenly, I whisper to her, "Please enjoy your moment and I'll return shortly with some water."

I leave the room and meet the focused eyes of Zune as she asks, "How did it go?"

"I'm not really sure."

"Good! You're learning."

Before I could return to the room with water, the woman appears with the cane in her hand, no longer needing its support. She smiles at both of us and simply comments to Zune, "As soon as he got out of his head, we got some work done!"

Zune replies, "Patience Eva. It's as much the age we live in as it is the youth of his age."

As Eva drinks her water, I return to the back room and straighten it up. Upon my return, Eva is gone. In the hour that follows, I relay my experience to Zune. She quietly sits and listens without interruption. Finally, I stop, having shared everything I could think to say. A silence takes over the room.

Zune's gaze overwhelms me now as she says, "Go now and focus on the words of your heart and not those of your head."

I stand up, bow to her, and leave in silence.

In the coming months, I see all types of clients

from all levels of society. The only thing they all have in common is their fear of being healed! Most often, a given client uses her situation to leverage attention from her inner circle of friends. But I can't really blame them. Most of the human condition is about one hundred and one ways to avoid growth in the world.

One day Zune simply says, "You're done; I can teach you no more. Forget all I've shared with you and begin to find your way." In that moment, I feel like I may never see her again. If there is a next time, neither she nor I will be the same.

Unexpectedly, about twenty clients later, Zune appears one day. She's intently focused as she asks, "How do you like the system of Reiki?"

I fall into thought for a moment as all my client sessions play back in my mind like a small-town parade. I replay my thoughts, feelings, and insights several times and discover a trend of concern as clear as day. I look deeply back into Zunes eyes and begin, "I don't support the notion of intention. In the first moment I scan someone, I have a clear sense of what's out of alignment. Normally, I create an intention to counter that dis-ease. Up to that point it's all good. But, in the next moment, I bring in the light and my client status changes! The original intention is now obsolete. So, the only thing I know to do is to get my head-based intention out of it altogether! To answer your question, I just open myself and let spirit work with the ever-changing status of the client in a dynamic way."

Zune looks at me carefully and says, "Yes, the

intention is really only for the result of healing and not the process of healing." She grabs my right hand and moves it to my heart saying, "The intention is for you dear one!"

Suddenly it makes perfect sense. My instincts have been right all along. I don't think I'll be using this modality very much longer, but it has been priceless to have an opportunity to refine and trust my own intuition.

I can tell Zune is about to leave when she knowingly says, "Ask it."

Of course, she's right in knowing I have a question. I start, "I have one more question that has dogged me since we first met. Zune, why or how did you know that Jonah would only need one more session the night we met? Jonah told me he got off the table that day and never felt better."

Zune smiles and picks up a stick off the ground. She draws two circles in the dirt. She points to the left circle saying, "This is you! At that time, you were orbiting in this area of space." Next, she points to the right circle saying, "This was me and my orbit. Notice that the two circles have a large gap between them." Next, she draws a third circle that overlaps my circle but not Zune's saying, "This was Jonah's circle before the burning car event." Now she adds a triangle that overlaps her and Jonah's circles saying, "This is the car event. In this case, the fire event altered both our paths and allowed Jonah and I to meet. This was part of our contract. More importantly, Jonah now allowed our two circles to connect through him. The moment we met, per Jonah's introduction, his contract with me was finished."

"More please."

She continues, "Jonah, on a soul level, would continue to exhibit pain symptoms to provide a need for treatment from me until we met. Again, after we met, he had fulfilled his contract to you and me. So, on a soul level, he no longer needed to maintain the pain symptoms. Jonah had contract-based pain!"

As I look down at the symbols on the ground, all I can do is shake my head in amazement. I never thought of the link between spirit and life to be so intertwined in a fabric of growth and expansion.

In the next moment, I look from the circles on the ground to the glow in Zune's eyes saying, "Is our contract done or will we meet again?"

She replies, "What does your intuition tell you?"

I first realize I'm looking in my head for the answer. Then, next I search within my heart. Finally, I move to that place of quiet knowing. It is there that I see Zune as a totally different being altogether as I say, "You are radiant, loving and knowing. You are Kara! We are in the beginning of our time here, not the end."

Zune's face is now lightly veiled with Kara's face and I'm not sure to whom I'm speaking. Graciously, Kara smiles and says, "Remember, Ease, this is my disguise this time around. Please continue to honor that I'm Zune in this here and now."

With that said, Kara's image fades away.

World-Side: Grace before a lecture

Grace refines the last of her notes before her lecture begins. There is uneasiness about the room that sends a chill up her arms as she looks out from behind the curtain to see people finding chairs and getting comfortable. Back and forth she scans the crowd and whispers to herself, "With heart!"

Suddenly, a few people in the audience begin to glow. I smile thinking, I love to see auras. It makes my job so much easier when I know the emotional state of who I'm talking to. I feel it's like cheating but this is one of my gifts.

With a bit more focus now, I'm able to see almost half of the crowd as a rainbow of color in every shade and clarity. Noticing as I scan, I'll bet that soul is a rocket science major. Look at that huge orb of yellow around her head. Oh, and look. I bet that girl just broke up. I'd recognize that shade of reddish lavender coming from her heart and the muddy blue in her throat anywhere. She's filled with so much emotion that she can't speak a word! Looking at my watch, I motion for the host to begin.

The host, a professional woman in her mid-fifties, begins, "Please have a seat. We're ready to begin. I'm so very pleased to have this opportunity to bring a pioneer of emotional heart research and expression to our campus. As most of you know, I was challenged on many levels with the passing of my husband of forty-two years. But by the grace of God, I found the woman who will now stand before you. She is a woman that at such a young age has mastered an understanding of her heart in both the world of men and women. So, with no further ado, I present to you, Grace Moore!"

I take the stage and feel the rush of curious focus from the crowd. After the polite applause subsides, I allow a moment of silence by simply saying, "Find your heart. Take a moment from your life's pursuits and find your heart. Open your hands and find your heart. Be one with all and find your heart."

The room becomes silent beyond measure. Now, I see the entire room of souls with countless shades of pulsing lavender radiating from their heart centers. Smiling I say, "Lovely! Now we can begin."

The crowd reacts with a deep breath and a little laugh. I begin, "I'm here by the grace of all to ask you to consider making peace between your body, head, and heart. Peace that will allow you to reclaim your soul's purpose."

Somehow, this wasn't what the crowd expected as they sat motionless and focused. I continue, "We, all of us, are both male and female, power and compassion, yin, and yang. We are both by design. It is this heavenly design that allows us to both expand and embrace ourselves and each other with every breath of our being. Today, we will find that breath again!"

Pre-Life: Voyor plans his first meeting with Mara

Today is full of anticipation for me. I've climbed this hill a thousand times. This hill, one of the seven sisters, overlooks most of the city of stars. But, more importantly it is our place. It is the special place where I come to meet Mara. It is a place beyond the universe that only we share.

As is our tradition, we stand nine feet apart with hands in exchange mode and effortlessly allow our energies to ebb and flow. During this exchange I ask Mara, "Have you thought any more about how you'd like to time our first meeting?"

Mara responds, "I have a few ideas Voyor. Are you looking for subtle, dramatic, or mysterious?"

Smiling I reply, "This is so special! I'm thinking…"

Mara says, "Yes you are!"

We both laugh. We have a long-standing joke about me leading interactions with my head rather than the whole of my being. Yet through all my growth, or lack of it, she has always remained kind. I say, "Ok, let's try this again."

I purposely allow my body, mind, heart, and soul to blend into a stream of knowingness. From that state, I arrive at an intention. The intention looks much like a beach ball of energy ebbing and flowing as it floats over to Mara and interacts with her field.

She smiles saying, "Ah, subtle, dramatic, and mysterious! How very romantically bold you are. I like it!" She continues, "So it sounds like some foreshadowing is in order. Are we still set on meeting at thirty-three?"

I answer, "Yes, at least in the conscious sense. What are your thoughts on our subconscious path?"

Mara reflects for a moment and notes, "I'd like a strong sense of knowingness from a near distance. I want to smell it, feel it, and almost touch it; touch us! Yet we must honor and afford Jade an opportunity to also blend within your field."

I simply state, "Agreed."

Our energy blending has changed to a lavender field with ribbons of violet, dancing and then changing to include the entire spectrum of the rainbow. In perfect unison, we say, "We are both ends of our rainbow! We are one!"

World-Side: Grace continues the lecture

As I continue to lecture, I'm aware of a soul sitting toward the back of the auditorium. His head center is a quiet but active shade of yellow within an overall field of green. I think to myself, "Wow, now that's one powerful healer! Looking closer, I notice how clear all his centers are. So very rare in this day and age of emotional-based distractions.

Bringing myself back to focus, I continue, "The very core of our heart's fear has nothing to do with each other, but of our untrusting view of self. In this moment, I, as a stranger, can say nothing to you that would hurt you in any way. Unless of course, you empower me to do so! So, you might now ask yourself, why would I ever empower anyone to hurt me?"

A dead silence falls over the room as I watch my mystery guy's heart center change from clear violet to pulsing clear lavender. Reflecting, I find that to be odd. I've never seen that before! Yet how absolutely refreshing that he's processing the information with his heart-felt soul!

Grace continues, "Further, remember you came into this life with contracts of authority given to those you chose to be your parents. But that was only in terms of narrowing your field of focus to your soul's highest purpose and good. Now, as adults, you are or can be in a state of heart-felt intention. So back to the question, 'Why do you empower any soul to hurt you?' The answer of course is you don't! You only empower yourself to hurt yourself via others! They are contracted to serve you. Why then would you choose to hurt yourself?"

I allow a pause and then continue, "You hurt yourself because you do not trust yourself to consistently embrace your highest spiritual purpose and good!"

World-Side: Ease finds himself at Grace's lecture

Wow, as I watch the guest speaker, I feel quite uneasy. I find myself wondering how I got here. I mean how weird is it to have a total stranger walk up to you, look you deeply in the eyes and hold out two tickets to this event, simply saying, "You need to go to this. It's important!"

I really didn't think much about it at the time

except for it being a great way to get Leah out of the lab so we could catch up. Of course, Leah is in another world of symbols and relationships these days. On the other hand, who isn't? I wish Leah was here right now. I about jumped out of my skin when the presenter spoke about contracts. She's sort of like Zune in a way, but different. I can't help but enjoy watching her aura as she speaks. She brings such a focus to her words and her truth is so heartfelt.

Grace continues, "It's time in our lives, in our age, in our being, to love ourselves first and foremost. Allow your inner guide to make the distinction between the self-fullness of light and the selfishness within the world. With that new shift, we can begin to reintegrate our love with the ability to create compassionate power. A power that is calm. A power that is kind. A power that is strength. Roosevelt said, 'The only thing to fear is fear itself,' and that's never been truer. Within each one of us is a frightened child. We are not afraid of the shadows of failure but rather the limitlessness of the true beings we all are! I ask you now, with your heart fully engaged, to awaken that power. Feel that power. Be the power that is your soul! Stand up. Raise your hands to the sky and feel the breath of true love flowing up and out into the world!"

I, like everyone in the crowd, rise to my feet with hands raised to the heavens and am in the moment. At first, I have my eyes closed but as my flow gets stronger, I feel as though I'm being touched by the speaker. Who is this woman, no older than me, who has such an understanding between power and love? Who is this woman they call Grace? She seems to be her name! Grace on Earth!

The lecture goes on for a while longer but I'm not really hearing much. My heart is pounding, and I can't take my eyes off her. Her aura is expanding beyond belief. She fills the hall with power and grace. No, with the power of grace! She's so effortless, I feel like I should know her. I feel like I do know her. We must have a contract. Yes, that's it! But a contract about what?

World-Side: Grace concludes the lecture

Vital and engaged, Grace enjoys the applause, thinking, "Wow, it's almost over, by the grace of heaven. I'm so very glad because my heart needs to understand why I can't stop looking at that soul. Sure, his aura is bright and clear, but I feel his eyes looking through me! How I can be so known and unknown to this being is beyond me. Yet there he is before my eyes. My heart pounds in a rhythm within my chest. May my soul's destiny grant that our paths cross this night!"

CHAPTER EIGHT

"...getting old doesn't serve me."

Pre-Life: Mara and Jade speak of their contract

AS JADE SMELLS a rose, she realizes that she hasn't been in this garden in a century, World-Side time. The hedges are neatly trimmed to form a maze upon which a soul might clear her heart space. Arbors frame the center with the fragrant aroma of roses in full bloom. A gentle brook carries lost petals to distant shores while serving to break the silence. It's incredibly beautiful and tranquil.

Mara should be here shortly. This will be the first time to speak with Mara outside of Voyor's soul pod. I've thought long and hard about our contract. How we might help each other and ourselves at the same time. I don't think I'll ever lose my desire to empower souls. I wonder how Voyor is doing with all this change before our final incarnations. We thought it was going to be so easy this time, so effortless and so much bliss. Now, it's like we don't know anything at all.

From behind me, I hear Mara approach. I turn and greet her with, "Thanks for sparing a moment for us to share. I'm feeling a bit outside looking in with Voyor's group. You've all been together so very long."

Mara stands with open arms as she and Jade hug for a long moment. Mara whispers in Jade's ear, "We can be quiet in this space with Voyor not here." They both laugh. Mara continues, "Please join me in sharing today," as she gestures for Jade to join her sitting on the ground.

Jade sits back-to-back with Mara and the two lean against each other. Mara leads them into a swaying motion that finds the rhythm of their hearts. Once their hearts are in rhythm, Mara stops the swaying. The two of them sit motionless for an exceptionally long moment when Jade suddenly giggles to break the mood. Mara giggles too as they leave the ground to sit on one of the benches.

Mara begins, "So tell me Jade, what is your primary goal for this coming life?"

Jade responds, "To complete the circle of my beingness with the passion to know everything! But it's more than that. It's to feel the knowing. Live the knowing. Know the knowing. But for the first time on my journey, I think, or rather feel, like there's something more! Much more! For the very first time it seems more about what and not the how."

Mara smiles and caresses Jade's hair. Jade lies down and places her head on Mara's lap.

Jade continues, "I feel so young and empty! What I thought I knew is nothing. I feel reborn again!"

Mara helps Jade sit up saying, "Trust me child, you know much and that's why you have come to us. I believe we have much to share but we are short on time. Let us speak of Voyor."

"Yes, let's."

Mara continues, "Voyor is that knowing we seek. He is a feeling, a joy, a longing to be whole. He has been before, so he knows of knowing. Yet his being is to share his light for all that ask. He is tireless in his desire to heal and empower with the depth of his soul's breadth. Yet too, he is the child that yearns to learn. You and I are the Yin to his Yang. We are the clouds of his sky, the moon to his sun and his hope of one…"

Jade begins to cry saying, "I don't understand! Why am I here? How can I be what you already are?"

Mara wipes a tear from Jade's face saying, "We are nothing. We are both seeds. We are a night with no day. We are a heart with no soul. We are a path with no choice!"

Jade looks deeply into Mara's eyes saying, "What can I do? Please guide me!"

Mara takes Jade's hand and begins, "The beginning will be the hardest of times when you must be true to your soul beyond the calling of your body. We will help you much with Starmarks, so you are reminded that in each trying moment you have a choice…"

World-Side: Ease at the end of Grace's lecture

The end of the lecture is more like a rock concert and Grace the accessible star. Hugs, tears, and autographs fill the moment. I stand there watching, waiting, hoping in some magical way that this incredible woman might see me and give me a moment to know her more!

Grace thinks to herself, "I can't believe it. There he is, just standing there! He's just standing, unmoving as I sign what seems to be countless programs. I must focus. I must be present. Souls have come to see me, and I must cherish each heart."

Just then, the host announces that Grace has agreed to stay a little longer and will receive members of the audience in the Union Room.

Ease smiles. Yes! There's my magic! I watch her move out of the hall and toward the Union Room with a collection of followers in tow. She seems to glance back once to meet my eyes, but is my imagination playing tricks on me? Time to find the Union Room! I'm in awe of the response she has gotten. She is a rock star, a rock star of heart!

Looks like I'm the last in a line of more than a hundred souls. Each one has a story to tell and a heart to heal. The line is moving very slowly yet, as each soul passes, the feeling within me grows. Like hands to a flame, my body burns with anticipation!

Grace glances up. Yes! There is magic! There he is. How perfect, he's the last in line. The last soul to know! I feel him like a torch in the night. His being shows as a light, a beacon, a glorious sight! My hands have begun to tingle, and my knees are weak. Just ten more souls and I'll know if this is wishful or perhaps true soul's gold.

Ease's palms tingle ever more. I can't take my eyes off her, but I don't care. Suddenly my eyes are covered by hands I know well. The words, "Guess who?" are whispered in my ear from a voice filled with joy. I take the hands in mine and feel the pulse of a racing heart. Leah moves close to spoon me. I feel the warmth of her body radiate through mine.

The moment is broken as a soul asks, "Are you the last one in line?"

Leah removes her hands and with a smile that could melt hearts says, "No, you are. We're just leaving." Leah takes my hand and pulls me away as I look back to see Grace greet the new last one in line.

Grace looks up briefly from that last soul and our eyes truly meet. Just then the fire alarm goes off, Grace covers her ears and Leah pulls me away. Once down the hall Leah says, "Wow, wicked bell. Sorry about the lecture. Did I miss anything? I hope it was light-hearted. You know how you get sometimes." It is obvious that Leah is in a great mood.

World-Side: As friends go, we're the best when we're together

Leah's mood reminds me more of when we were in college than I've seen her in years. The passion is the same, but the focus is on me. As we rush out of the building, Leah turns and says, "I've missed you so much. We've got to make time more often."

I laughed in knowing how much I've tried to get together for years with the same result every time. Leah would cancel at the last minute with the same reason. I can hear her time and again saying, "I'm close to something big. Just not sure what it is." For her, it's out of sight, out of mind. Thinking back, I almost wish I'd never taken her on that picnic and suggested that she redirect her passion. I wish I'd never hesitated to share that kiss!

As friends go, we're the best when we are together. We cuddle, snuggle, and hug a lot. But a kiss on the cheek always ends the night. Yet most times I feel that I want to explore her and long to know of the love that she holds in her heart and the passion in her soul.

Tonight, is different somehow. We dance, sing, and skip in the park. In a quiet moment, Leah shares that she and her team have made a breakthrough that will change the future of plastics. I know she can't say much so I don't ask a thing. Nevertheless, a profound burden seems to be gone from her now.

It's late as we find ourselves in front of Leah's apartment. She invites me in, starts a fire, hands me a drink and leaves to change clothes. Wow. What a weird night for me. Again, my heart is pounding to an unknown rhythm. First it was at the lecture to a woman I almost met and now for a woman my heart yearns to know. Leah returns and we spoon silently in front of the fire for a long while. Suddenly, she rolls over and sits up. She looks very closely at my face and then even closer at my eyes. Amazed, she exclaims, "You don't have any wrinkles. None! How can that be? Everyone has wrinkles."

World-Side: "Getting old doesn't serve me"

I smile, giggle, and laugh saying, "Well Leah, getting old doesn't serve me. So, I just stopped aging."

Leah knows I tend to exaggerate sometimes so she asks, "How? How exactly? What do you use?"

I sit up to face her and begin, "About seven years ago I did some soul searching and realized I wasn't where I wanted to be in my life. My body was great, but my career was behind schedule. I'd always wanted to be a young millionaire so that I could enjoy and celebrate my youth."

"Don't we all!"

"My dilemma was how can I stop aging and let my career catch up. Then I happened to run across a fun fact on the internet about cells. It seems that almost all the cells in our body regenerate every seven years. Then I thought about the stages our body goes through and that growth seems to be based on seven-year cycles as well. So, I did some more exploring and realized that our world's social progression also mirrors the seven-year cycle."

"At the time, I began wondering about the fourth cycle from age twenty-one to twenty-eight. For the most part, we've completed our growth phase at twenty-one. Our DNA has executed its coding and we are what we are. Old isn't a factor when you're twenty-one!"

Leah comments, "Ah yes, the good old days." She gently feels the wrinkles on her face. I continue, "Then I ran into Jonah, and he invited me over to his new place. It wasn't new at all. It was a fixer-upper in a big way. When I got there, I saw the bare frame of a house with piles of scrap wood everywhere. In the middle of it all was Jonah and his architect looking intently at a set of blueprints. Jonah excitedly motioned for me to come over and see the plans."

Leah stops me saying, "Wait! What's a remodeling job got to do with not aging?"

I continue, "We're almost there. Okay, so I went over to them as they pointed again and again at the plans. Having done so, I watched as Jonah and the architect spoke of moving this wall to here and that wall to there. Then I noticed that some of the walls were color-coded and asked why. The architect said as a matter of course that everything in white is the original design. The blue section is the first revision. The green is the second revision, and the red is what they're planning now. I asked, 'Okay, why all the changes?'"

"He answered, 'It's all about keeping up with the Joneses. It's all about being unique but keeping pace with the neighborhood. Most of the work will be cosmetic changes.'"

"It was in that moment that I felt struck by lightning! It was so clear. We, each of us, start with a clean clear blueprint that is unique and functional for the first twenty-one years. We grow into the space, and all is well. Unlike houses however, your body rebuilds itself, not all at once, but rebuilds itself all the same. The question is what set of plans do we choose to build from? Remember that we grow into ourselves up to age twenty-one. So, the question is, 'What set of plans will we use for the rebuilding from twenty-two to twenty-eight?' In theory, if we don't modify the original plans, then at the end of seven years our bodies will look and be the same as they were at twenty-one!"

"That's what I did. I just didn't know it at the time. I focused on the original design. I didn't care one bit about keeping up with the gang. I didn't care about maturing or filling out. My body at twenty-one was and would be my plan until further notice!"

Leah adds, "I get it! It's all so very simple."

"Now, you know better than I that we are what we eat, and that holding stress depletes oxygen. But, with all this in mind, I just can't think of a reason to age at all!"

Leah makes a pouting face, "All good for you, but I'm seven years in the wrong direction! How do I turn back time?"

Thinking for a moment I respond, "Get a great headshot from when you were twenty-one. Cut away the hair style and jewelry so that all you see is your face. Then, every morning, invest in remembering who you were, how you felt, and what you dreamed of doing."

"Zen out and be twenty-one again! Now please understand this is not about you looking in the mirror and comparing yourself to the picture. That would just make you crazy. This is about reprograming the execution of your DNA blueprint."

Leah's eyes fill with excitement as she says, "So how long will it take?"

I look into her eyes as if to project the answer into her head and say, "You're the chemist, you tell me." Leah is thinking as I add, "Remember this is a simple process that the body does with no conscious effort on our part. It is an automatic process."

Leah's face changes from curious to knowing as she feels her face again and says, "Seven years!"

Joyfully I shout, "You got it! Rock on! Time to turn back time! Back to the past!"

We high-five and then hug. She feels so good in my arms. I feel like a kid at Christmas that just got his favorite toy. The hug slowly begins to change as I feel energy starting to flow up my spine. The passion of my quiet soul is now adding to my fire. I've longed, dreamed, and hoped to be with Leah! It's all so perfect. It's all so right!

World-Side: A moment with Leah

The past and the future fall away, leaving us in our now. Leah gently leans both of us to the floor. I feel the length of her body on mine. She moves her face back and forth against mine. Her soft skin is like silk to the touch. Slowly, she rises, and I feel all her weight shift to my hips. Leah, with hands on the sides of my face, carefully and silently looks deeply at me. I feel like she is looking through me. Her gaze fuels my passion. With each breath it grows stronger. I flash to all those times we almost kissed. Those moments that seemed to be beyond time.

I have a sense of being part of a whole. Ever so slowly, she leans down. Her lips are wet and glistening in the light of the fire. Her breath excites my skin. The weight of her body now meets my chest. The power of our being rushes over me like a wave crashing into the rocky shore. I am both exhilarated and fearful. I am impassioned and hesitant. My fire becomes me. Her lips, those that I've longed to touch, to taste, to become one with, are upon me. I know no edges. They have all left me. Where do I start? Where does she end? My thoughts now flee from my head. There is just her, me, and we as her phone rings!

The trance is broken, and I return to my body. Leah is back too with a frustrated but excited look on her face. She quickly plants a kiss on my forehead and rises to answer her cell. Now back in my body, I'm still unable to move. I feel her weight still on me but she's no longer there. The essence of her spell now escapes me. As she talks, I begin to feel the heat radiating from the fire again and begin to wiggle my fingers and toes. My head is numb and still unable to hold thought.

Leah begins to hop up and down, so I know it's

something good. She hangs up as I slowly get up off the floor, still unsettled from the moment. She shares, "Ease you'll never believe what happened. The lab just finished with my phase three testing, and the project is all a go! It will be a snap to get funding now! I'm so excited! How many years has it been?"

Thinking for a moment, I say, "Let's see, it's been seven years since you got your bachelor's degree. There's that number again."

Leah reflects a moment and pouts, "I'm so sorry about the call but I've been waiting for this news for weeks now."

Shaking my head, "Yes, waiting seems to be a challenge for all of us! It sure has been a weird day today with all the alarms and bells. What are the odds?"

Leah throws on some sweats, "I'm sorry but I must go finish up a few things in the lab before morning. You understand." With a bit of urgency, she hands me my coat and shows me to the door. Leah is thoughtful for an awkward moment about whether to kiss but then simply smiles and says, "Good night."

As I turn away and the door closes behind me, I flash back to the fire alarm at the lecture and the phone call just now. No, I really don't understand what's happening but I'm very sure that something has certainly happened!

CHAPTER NINE

"I'm talking about a spiritual relationship not a worldly one."

Pre-Life: Perspective of truth

I WAS THE last one to join my soul pod for our next session. I can see from entering the chamber that Lorna is very excited about our topic. Senior opens with, "Laughter, love, and light to you this fine moment. Today we will continue our exploration of the perspective of truth."

Lorna immediately states, "Truth is beyond perspective. It simply is!"

Senior smiles as she opens a study port centered about our table saying, "As the lesson displays, each of you will view the sequence of events from a different perspective, similar to Voyor's example of the ball and flame we studied earlier."

An electronic mist fills the air and forms an event

opening in a place called Venice Beach in southern California, World-Side. It's a sunny morning in front of a sidewalk café. Across the way, two musicians are setting up to play. People pass between in a carefree way. Senior stops the event and addresses the group, "Now two of you will observe from the musicians' point of view, which I'll call POV, for short. One of you, Mara I think, will observe from a local homeless soul's POV. Lorna will view from a frustrated local's POV. Voyor will observe from the very beginning of the event as a customer in the café. The rest of you will view from the café as well but starting mid-event."

Senior now advances the event. The musicians begin to play their first set as the café patrons go about ordering and eating breakfast. All is peaceful and calm. About three songs later, Mara's male character walks into the scene and is immediately captured by the music. He delights with pure joy as he dances and moves to the melodic sound. The patrons also remember a time in their lives when their inner child allowed them to express such simple joy.

The song concludes and it is obvious that the homeless man is truly moved. He reaches into his pockets to find a few coins totaling seventeen cents. He searches his pockets again to find nothing more. Gratefully, he bows and tenderly places the coins in the musician's bowl. Beaming and joyful, he bows again and dances away.

A few souls in the café are moved to witness this act of appreciation which shines so brightly on the musicians' faces. The musicians begin to play again but a bit more upbeat this time. As the energy between the café and the musicians begins to build, a second local soul rides by on a very old bike. He slows a bit to listen to the song.

At this point, Senior notes that the rest of the group is now to enter the café and be seated next to Voyor. The local soul now rides back and forth and his expression changes like night and day. When he looks at the musicians he smiles with joy. When he turns his head back to the café he sneers. This pattern continues until the song comes to an end. At that point the man walks his bike up to the musicians' bowl and looks down to see the seventeen cents.

In the next moment, he flies into a fit of rage! He picks up the bowl, grabs the coins and shouts to the café crowd, "You selfish sons of bitches! You goddamn cheap bastards! How the hell do you think we eat down here?" Back and forth he rides his bike, swearing each time he reaches the crowd. The patrons, all now aware of his rage, watch his final act as he throws the coins at the crowd, pulls a wad of singles out of his pocket, and places a crumpled dollar in the bowl.

The musicians and crowd are taken aback at the display of anger they have just witnessed. Thankfully, the moment is broken when the musicians begin to play, and the crowd again settles back to eating. Soon after, the musicians finish their first set and grateful patrons contribute to a passed bowl.

Senior freezes the event and asks, "How many truths are present during the course of the event?"

Lorna shouts out, "Four!"

Senior asks, "And they are?"

Lorna continues, "One was the musicians. Two was the first homeless guy. Third was the bike guy and the fourth was the people in the café."

Senior continues, "All right, based on four, was the crowd 'cheap' as the angry man stated? All those who were in the café perspective speak first."

Freemar begins, "Seventeen cents was a bit insulting. I see the angry man's point of view."

Senior asks, "Mara, your thoughts."

Mara smiles and raises her hands to her heart, "The first homeless man is so beautiful, so giving and so full of love! He gave everything he had to honor the musicians' expression and they knew that as well, in addition to all the patrons in the café that witnessed the act."

Senior asks, "From the musicians' point of view was the crowd cheap?"

Lor and Kara look at each other and say, "We're not sure."

Senior responds, "Great! Why don't you know?"

Kara continues, "They gave at the end of the set but not at the end of the songs."

Voyor adds, "From my perspective, I know that the crowd never gives until the end of the set so for me there were five truths. The fifth truth reflects the passing of time. The first four and a knowing that there were four was in fact the fifth!" Finishing my statement, I look at Lorna and she at me. Within our gaze, we both grow closer to mastering our perspective of knowing universal truth.

World-Side: "You're never going to believe this!"

Grace is busy answering the last email from last month's lecture. Two hundred and fifty-six emails have been a bit overwhelming. I guess I'll have to come up with a better system. Each time I speak, I receive a larger response. Each email is so precious to me. I learn so much from the messages I receive.

Just then, Marshal enters the room with a piece of paper in hand saying, "Grace, you're never going to believe this! Your agent just called. You've been invited to be the keynote speaker at next year's conference! That's just so awesome! We did it! You did it!"

Grace reflects, "This is going faster than I'd ever guess in a million years."

Marshal responds, "I don't know why you're so surprised. You speak from the heart! You live from your heart. You are your heart!"

She sighs, "Hearing that is great if I could just find someone to share it with."

Struggling to stay calm, Marshal comforts her saying, "You'll find that special someone." Time seems to slow a bit for Marshal as he reflects on the years he has spent at Grace's side. He thinks, "How long has it been? All of nine years, I guess." He feels so close to her, yet a million miles away as he says, "You'll find him, I just know it."

"What about that guy you saw at the lecture? Did he email you?"

Grace shakes her head, "I don't know. It was so confusing. I felt like we were the only two souls in the room. Time all but stopped. We were about to meet when a woman came out of nowhere, the fire alarm went off and he was gone! I don't know anything about him except that I feel like I know everything about him."

"You are such a romantic, darling." He comes up behind Grace, begins to massage her shoulders and whispers, "You'll find your soul. You'll find the truth of your heart. I have faith!"

"Yes, but I'm not sure what's supposed to happen when I do."

"What do you mean? It's simple, you'll meet, fall madly in love, get married, have kids and the rest is history!"

Grace pulls away, "Marshal, you don't get it! Haven't you been listening to my lectures? You of all souls should know about the truth of love!"

World-Side: World vs. spiritual relationships

Focusing intently Grace begins, "Love is about empowerment now! Our parents' and grandparents' notion of love and marriage no longer serves our souls. It's about the truth of love! It's about the soul we are, not the roles we play! We must love ourselves first to set the standard by which others honor us."

Marshal resorts to a grade school approach by raising his hand, "Ok, you lost me. That sounds a little selfish."

"Not selfish but rather self-full."

"I'm still not following."

Motioning him to sit down, Grace declares, "Okay, let's start at the beginning. From a spiritual perspective, we come into the world for one reason, to evolve our souls. That's our pure truth. As much as I might want to, I can't do one thing to expand you and you really can't do one thing for me. You can't take a single step on my journey."

Marshal replies, "Go on."

"Okay, so here I am down here growing, exploring, and expanding. One day I meet someone that complements me. Now remember that our primary purpose is to evolve our souls. So, if we both honor ourselves then what can we really bring to the table? In the purest sense of truth, we can make no promises to the other or to ourselves without compromising our own growth. So, in truth, we can only offer each other an intention to be consistently and compassionately interested in sharing experiences on each other's journeys. That's it! Anything else would be a lie. It is those kinds of lies that become a guilt-ridden shackle upon which to punish and bind ourselves."

Marshal shakes his head in confusion, "But what kind of relationship is that? How can that work in the world?"

Grace smiles, "It can't. I'm talking about a spiritual relationship not a worldly one. Think about it. How can I promise to be here or there and still address his needs if my soul's journey requires me to jump on a plane and spend a year in Egypt? Why set up a platform for expectation and guilt. Where is the truth in that kind of deal?"

Marshal shakes his head again, "Good luck with that!"

"What do you mean?"

"I mean, I get it. It might look good on paper, but I don't see that as being very attractive."

Grace firmly says, "You, I, and the world need to change our notion of what a relationship is about. If we can just get back to how we support each other as best friends, then we will have a good start. Think about it. Most of the great marriages you know started as best friends. Friends that are passionate about watching each other grow. No agenda, no fear, just a consistent passionate support of growth. They never think of changing each other, they just watch each other change." Taking a breath, Grace sits down and sighs.

Marshal thinks for a moment before saying, "Wow, that's a beautiful vision! I get it! But until now, I've never thought of it in those terms. Every woman I know is still in princess mode. They are focused on big weddings, houses, and bills. That's about as far from empowerment and encouraging another soul as you can get!"

Grace sighs, "Yes, I know."

"So, what makes you think that this guy is any different than every other guy in the world?"

Grace sits up, "His aura! His power of being!"

"But you didn't even meet him. I don't understand."

"Look, I've told you before about seeing auras. That's how I know how you're feeling before you do most of the time."

Marshal reacts, "Hey, you need to stop doing that! That's not fair. I don't try to read you. I just try to be present. There are days when I know you're working through something but it's not for me to add to or change your focus."

"You're so right! You've been such a great friend to me for so many years and deserve to process your own stuff on your own terms. I guess that's just something I picked up as a girl. My dad used to drink a lot. So, the sooner I knew what mood he was in, the more time I had to vanish. It's funny how we develop our gifts from situations that are far from love."

"Okay, back to Mister Right."

Grace playfully hits Marshal on the arm saying, "Stop! Okay, when I was standing there at the end of the lecture his centers were clearer than anyone I've ever seen. No cloudy or muddy veil. They were just pure clean color. As I would speak from one of my centers he would respond with the same. Time after time he responded immediately to the movement of my energy. Finally, as I was about to end the lecture, he reached out from his heart chakra as if to bond to me in some way. It was a feeling of fitting. A feeling of being more than the sum of us! I have never ever felt that way before."

"Do you think he felt the same way?"

"In some magical way, I don't see how he couldn't!"

"So, what are you going to do?"

Grace looks a bit blank, "I don't know. I have no way of knowing who he is or if he's even able to meet."

Curiously, Marshal asks, "What do you mean able to meet?"

Grace shows a bit of concern in her voice, "He was with another woman, and she had incredible energy too!"

With insight Marshal adds, "Sounds like you're relatively concerned about this. What happened to allowing everyone their journey?"

"I just don't know! I understand spiritual love but understanding it and living it are two different things!"

Marshal adds, "Well if anyone in the world deserves the love of a lifetime it's you Grace!" They hug and Marshal adds, "I guess for now we'll just have to let spirit make some magic. Of course, the best thing you've got going for you is his aura. Sounds like you're not going to have any problem picking him out of a crowd."

Pre-Life: Voyor and Freemar in the garden

Voyor lies on the ground in a yin yang garden far above the city. A pair of birds fly in circles, gently framed by the fleeting clouds of a sunny summer day. I love watching the birds and clouds in the dance of now. It frees my mind and allows me to think of nothing at all. Sensing another presence, I sit up and feel the tingle of the densers on my arms and legs.

Just below, behind, and still a distance away, Freemar is climbing up to join me. I continue to wiggle my feet and arms as if to shake something off when I say, "Okay Freemar you can join me now, if you like."

A bit amazed, Freemar says, "Wow you're good. How did you know I was there?"

"I can feel you and see you in my mind's eye. It's so funny that on World-Side, souls are so reluctant to believe they have psychic abilities. Yet the moment they focus on someone, they appear in that person's mind. It's sort of like a psychic cell phone." We both laugh.

Freemar asks, "What did you want to speak with me about, my dear friend?"

"I've asked you here because, beyond all others in the group, you have explored the art of choice."

Freemar smiles, "Yes indeed. A few lifetimes would be an understatement. How can I help you?"

Pre-Life: The art of choice

Voyor begins, "Of course you know that I spoke for all of us when I found myself confused about Jade joining the group. It amazes me how a soul could have come to this place and time with such a different journey than the one we've shared."

Freemar responds, "I don't know. I'm not surprised at all. There is a true splendor within the Universe my friend. No matter where you go, there you are! And no matter where you are, you can go!"

"What does that mean?"

"Okay, remember back a few lifetimes ago when you and Mara chose to incarnate into that World-Side war. What was that? The Civil War, I think. I never understood how you can name a war 'civil'. Anyway, all sides were experiencing great loss and Mara, as a slave, was in your charge. You could have done anything to her at the time with no social recourse. Yet when faced with killing her you thought you could not. You felt like you didn't have a choice. Yet we always have a choice! There is always this way and that way."

"You and Mara have planned and complemented your journeys since your very beginnings. Why is that? From Mara's perspective, I'm in awe of her vision of love. She is the Venus of the Universe and yet she finds balance between the love of you and the love for you."

"You, on the other hand, know of the potential in each breath of expansion that there does in fact exist 'the way'. You understand that there is an approach to expanding that allows for perfect efficiency. You see a path that leads you to ascension the quickest. The notion of this efficiency drives the wheels of your choice! In every waking moment, souls on World-Side struggle, anguish, and torment about which path is the most effective. Which one is the most compassionate? Which one is the quickest? The paradox here is that unless you could see the maze of choices, there's no way to know."

"Yet, we think this series of choices is almost impossible in the world of men. Think in this moment of the statement 'All roads lead to Rome'. We could change that to 'Every road must lead us to Rome' and we would still be correct! Each twist and turn must lead to our goal. The only difference is the passing of time. Because we are not governed by time, we will always reach our destination. The question is not if, but when. If we continue our effort in any endeavor, we are certain to succeed. With that in mind, let's look at the process of how we proceed."

"It is a simple process of being fully present to where you are. Remembering where you came from. Understanding how fast you're going and the intention of where you want to go. Think of a race car driver. They do not plan each turn of the steering wheel. The great drivers simply are present and choose. It is those who hesitate who are truly lost. They are lost in reflecting on the past and stumbling blindly into the future."

"That is why so many souls make use of crashes in World-Side. With a crash they can, beyond social opinion, choose to stop. Stop the cycle of reaction in favor of moving through life with response."

Voyor asks, "Can you give me another example?"

Freemar continues, "Sure. Remember what it was

like to navigate a ship in the thirteenth century World-Side? There you are, out at sea. To move forward you absolutely need to know where you currently are! You need to be in your now. The stars assist you because the stars don't change with current events."

"The next thing of importance is the current we're in. Currents are physical limits that affect all of us equally. Then comes the wind to fill our sails. The wind is mostly like social ebb and flow. Even better, the wind is like social fads. A soul needs to be willing to understand social trends as opportunities to navigate forward to make choices that align with that trend. The worth of a culture is not solely defined by trends. Rather, it is defined by the longevity of those trends."

"The next three aspects reflect knowing ourselves. First, how are you built? Are you a racing yacht built for speed? Are you a wide hull built to carry large loads? Or are you in the middle as an explorer built for both? The last two aspects are very personal. The first aspect is what cargo are you carrying? Is your hull full of goods? In this case, goods would be memories. Or are you carrying only food and fuel?"

"Finally, how are your sails set? Are they full on with the wind so that you can get from point A to point B as fast as you can? Are you moving slowly to chart unknown waters? Or are you trimmed to allow for the smoothest ride?"

Pre-Life: Grace and Ease

Voyor interjects, "Wow, that's quite revealing. So, if I understand you, efficiency is more about the *way* we go through life, not how fast we go through life."

"Yes! If souls would simply look only to the quality of the experience they wish to have, and not compare it to anyone else, then they would maximize their experience. Thus, they would support their own perfection of their choices! It's only when they constantly change their moral compass that they invite in demons of doubt. Remember Voyor, it's all about grace and ease!"

Voyor exclaims, "That's amazing! That's it! You're brilliant beyond words my friend! Grace and ease! Grace and Ease! Mara and I have been contemplating names for World-Side and you, my friend, have delivered them to us through an effortless act of wisdom. I can't wait to share this with Mara. She is the grace of love!"

Freemar adds, "And you my friend are the ease of knowing!"

CHAPTER TEN

"... I Will be the Hell and Measure of your Faith!"

World-Side: Zune looks over the card spread

MAYBE THREE TIMES a year I go to Zune for a general Tarot reading. It's a good way for me to take a step back and listen to spirit. Zune sits silently looking over the spread of cards on the table as I watch. It's been four years since I saw the woman at the lecture. Yet she continues to appear in my mind and in my readings. Zune has been firm at times regarding seeking her out, but my passion will not be moved.

Zune looks up, "I really shouldn't continue to charge you for the same information. Your reading hasn't changed in years or should I say between fears. What are you waiting for? You have two women in your future. Why do you wait?"

Looking at Zune, I reply as I have for years, "The timing doesn't feel right. I can't justify it. I don't understand it. It's just something in my knowing. It's beyond me. Yet it is me!"

Zune looks closely at me, "Fair enough, it is always important to trust your knowing beyond all else."

Pre-Life: Voyor and Kara speak of a core part of their contract

Voyor passionately says, "Ok Kara, this has got to be one of the core pieces of our contract! You must do everything you can to take me away from my knowingness and the trust I have of it."

"But why? You have evolved this gift since your beginnings. What additional proof do you require?"

"I must go beyond my knowing. I must be my knowing! Since this is our final World-Side, it is for me and for us to know and trust myself beyond any measure of emotion. Nothing short of this will do. It is the foundation of all I am. So, please promise me that you will tirelessly attempt to sway me in the final years before Mara and I meet."

Kara asks, "Your plan is to meet at thirty-three?"

"Yes, that is correct."

"So, from the first time we meet until you reach thirty-three could exceed a hundred times!"

I nod, "Yes Kara, yes."

Kara shakes her head saying, "Because I love you so, my dear friend, I will be the hell and measure of your faith!"

World-Side: Zune challenges Ease

Zune looks me squarely in my eyes, "But I too must be true to my knowing, and I say your time is now!"

As I look back at her, I am struck by the moment more than any other in this life with an internal conflict. How do I step outside myself in this matter? I have known Zune for many years now. She is my mentor. She is my guide. She is my friend. But what is infinitely frightening is that, to date, she has never been wrong about anything! Could her heart sway her vision in this matter or is this all about me? How do I know? Is this my own blind spot?

Zune asks me to sit up straight, close my eyes and breathe like she has had me do a thousand times before. She begins, "Drift into yourself, Ease. Drift deeper, deeper, and still deeper to a place in your past. Go to this place of no fear. Feel a light breeze touch your face. Hear the water of a stream joyfully passing by. Taste the lingering of a fine wine. See wispy clouds pass above. Smell the fragrance of roses in bloom. Know that you are safe here. Know that you are loved. Breathe in deeply, look around you and see who is there. Who is sharing this moment with you? Who is the love of your life?"

I am no longer my current self. Time seems to have stopped somehow as I watch a butterfly slowly flap its wings to the song of the wind. Hundreds and hundreds of beautiful butterflies now fill my view. The sun shows through a single cloud to reveal the silhouette of a woman who feels that sun. Raising her hands upward, the butterflies part like waves of love that bow at her feet. She is my love. She is my being. She is me.

Zune now interjects, "As the cloud passes, the butterflies begin to part; her face begins to come into the light. Who is she?"

I look up as the shadows travel up her body and only a glow surrounds her face.

Zune again asks, "Who is she?"

I look again upon this goddess of love and reach up to touch her as she softly says with words that float on the wind, "Soon my love. We'll meet so very soon."

And with that my vision of her fades away...

My entire body sighs as the breath of my heart leaves me. I finally answer Zune's question with, "I don't know!"

I fall back in the chair feeling defeated in some way, but that smell! That smell still lingers! It's like a chorus of hundreds of different roses joining to become one. I'm in the stream of a scent that ebbs and flows within my mind's eye.

The look on Zune's face reveals questions and concern, "Ease, I am at a loss as to the nature of this woman. For I too saw only her silhouette! It feels much like a contract from long ago, yet new with the passion of first love. But how can that be? My vision still holds that your time is now and to that vision I must be true. But please continue to look within for your answers in the quietness of your heart and all will be revealed."

As always, I thank Zune with a long hug and silently depart with the scent of roses still lingering within me.

World-Side: Dinner with Leah tonight

I'm excited to have dinner with Leah tonight. I was surprised that she remembered my birthday but that makes it even more special. She didn't say where she was taking me which adds even more to the moment. Hmm! She said dress formally and be ready a bit before eight for a very important date. I laughed at the rhyme but am amazed that she used the "D" word.

Dating fell out of Leah's vocabulary during our senior year of college as she redirected her passion to chemistry. I guess it's been eleven years now. Wow, time has flown like the blink of an eye. Looking at myself in the mirror, I straighten my tie and note that not aging looks good on me! My admiration is interrupted with a knock on the door.

I open it to see a young soul waiting to deliver a boutonniere. I tip the girl as she comments, "Wow, someone must really like you very much to ship this rose in for you. It only grows in Maui. Have a special night!"

As she walks away, I'm silent as I hold the single rose. Carefully, I open the box and release the scent that fills me. I seem to be nowhere yet everywhere at the same time. In my mind's eye, I watch Leah finish the last touches to her look. Radiantly, she smooths her rich red dress along the line of her curves. Shaking her head, her hair falls to perfection. Then slowly and thoughtfully she applies lipstick that perfectly matches the rich lavender of the rose in my hand.

A surge of passion runs up my spine charging each cell as it passes. I am alive yet frozen in time. I drift back to a memory of a moment. The moment I looked up at Leah from the floor of my dorm room races back to me. I feel her smile and her eyes pass effortlessly through me. My heart longs to share the rhythm of hers. Her hand, like light, reaches out to me as I in turn reach out to meet hers. In an angel's tone, I hear again, "Hello to you. My name is Leah."

My hand relaxes and the rose begins to fall toward the floor. At once, I fire back into my body and respond instantly to the moment at hand. Quickly, effortlessly, and knowingly I snatch the rose before it hits the floor. The act has brought me to the present moment, with the memory of meeting Leah now drifting away. And with that, I'm safe to ponder what in the world does this all mean?

I reach for my cell phone and see it's four minutes to eight. With Zune's schedule so full these days, I'm hoping that she is free to speak. I need a moment and just a few words of encouragement to guide my way. The ring tone of the cell continues to sound but Zune does not answer.

Reluctantly, I hang up filled with a touch of fear.

Back at Zune's place, she gazes at her cell that

shows my name and smiles, saying quietly to herself, "Our contract is done!"

I think to myself, "Steady my friend," as I realize that I'm still standing in the hall. I gather myself and go back to the mirror not sure who might look back. Silently, I gaze at the form in front of me, studying each line in my face. Slowly, I feel the passing of time and choose to be all. Yes, all of thirty-three!

World-Side: The mystery ride

My phone rings and I answer to find that a town car has arrived to take me away. I'm still amazed at the effort Leah has made for me tonight. Somehow, I chose this, so I'll allow it to be all about me tonight! Once downstairs, the chauffeur opens my door and I enter the car. I notice his name tag reads Chance. I comment, "What an unusual name. Is Chance your real name?" He replies, "Yes, it is. I was my parents' third and last effort to have a second child. All the doctors thought that I wouldn't survive the night I was born, but here I am, still kicking." As we drive, Chance keeps looking at me from his mirror and notices the rose on my lapel. Finally, he smiles and says, "Wow what a beautiful rose! Man, you're a lucky guy. Whatever you're doing, I wouldn't change a thing!"

"What do you mean?"

"I've been in this business a long time and I've never seen a woman so passionate and detailed about creating an experience."

Shaking my head in agreement, I ask, "Where are we going?"

With a smile, he replies, "I can't say but we'll be there soon."

We're headed somewhere downtown, that's for sure but exactly where remains a mystery. An urgent feeling comes over me to look in a newspaper for some information. So, I ask, "Chance? May I call you Chance? Do you have a newspaper I might see?"

"Yeah, sure. That's perfect because we're running into some traffic from the big event downtown."

"Big event? What event?"

"I don't remember exactly: You and love. It's all about love. Love and something. It's supposed to be this love expert lecturing from out of town for charity. It costs a thousand dollars a plate! Boy that better be some really fine steak!"

I open the paper near the "Social and Event" section. As I turn the next page, I instantly feel a jolt run through my body. It's like touching bare wires. My whole-body tingles as I see a full page of a face looking back at me with the caption: "You too can find true love!"

"Oh my God! Is that the woman I saw on stage years ago?" I think to myself. It's streaming back to me. I remember the lecture, her aura and that dammed fire alarm! Suddenly, an emergency vehicle headed the other direction turns on its flashers and siren as another surge of energy rolls up my spine. Flashing lights of red and white reflect on the face in the newspaper and that face is Grace!

Pre-Life: Mara & Voyor discuss details

Upon our hill, one of the Seven Sisters, we find ourselves again. My eyes open slightly to see Mara's form as we continue to blend our energies. Over thousands of World-Side years, she has managed to continually refine her shell to reflect her mastery. Nature itself has fallen under her spell. No creature under the sun can resist joy upon seeing her face. She is strong yet accessible. She is firm but kind. She is a walking love beyond all of time.

Mara smiles and says, "No peeking," as she opens her eyes to see my gaze. "And to what do I owe the honor of your gaze this moment my dear Voyor?"

"You see through me once again! My heart betrays me to the beauty that is you."

"But my beauty in this moment of bliss is indeed a reflection of you!"

Our blending now surges tenfold as any soul within knowing of us stops, looks, and smiles. Each soul, in its own way, feels its own love through the flow of ours.

Mara lovingly speaks, "It's time to talk of details for our upcoming journey, dear Voyor. Have you given this thought since your group has changed to include Jade?"

"Yes and no. Jade is a paradox to the journey. To our journey. To the way of us."

Mara adds, "Perhaps to your notion of our journey but not to mine. For me, she is part of all that is. All is perfect with her and me. Both of us reflect you in every way. No matter whom you choose, all is right, all is true, and all is love."

My heart at this moment is torn by the same love that has forever set it free. A love that freed me to explore the depths of my soul and always know we would somehow be whole! Mara moves to me and places her hand on my heart. I feel the truth of her love guide me back to a place of calm.

A long moment later, I finally speak, "I wish our crossing on World-Side to be fair. I wish it to reflect the wonder of you. Yet I am bound to my journey to master choice. In the light of my mastery of knowing, I have no course!"

Mara again radiates into my heart the calm I do suddenly miss and says, "Perhaps you might explore the two paths separately at first and then consider the one. Start with Jade and speak of love. Embrace her passion and become her one. See love's depth and her passion through fun."

"Then, freed from time itself, embrace our journey of timeless wealth. Feel me then within your soul and all the pain for us will go. Remember our vision along the way and truth of love will bring forth our new day. Truth of love will find a way!"

I find the calm again and begin, "It is vital that we know our choices are upon us. So great is our quest that it must light the sky…"

World-Side: Ease is still in traffic

Chance makes a call to report that traffic is moving even slower than expected only to find out we still are on schedule. Commenting to that effect he says, "Wow, who is this woman? Is she a rocket scientist or something? She seems to have thought of everything!"

I smile, "Yes, she is sort of a rocket scientist. It's all about action and reaction in her world. Never a dull moment!"

We now enter through the gates and up the drive to the Museum of Fine Arts. Countless limos wait in line on a perfect summer evening. As cars move slowly forward, a full moon begins to rise and silhouette a few stray clouds in the night sky.

Finally, I'm beginning to enjoy the mystery of the moments ahead. Chance pops a bottle of champagne saying, "This is part of Plan B. I am to pour you a glass of champagne if we're not at the front entrance by eight forty-eight."

I take the glass slowly and can't help but notice the bubbles forming, releasing, racing to the top of the glass, and then exploding into the air. Champagne is such a perfect design to tickle your nose and bring you into the present moment. Somehow this feels like it could be my moment.

CHAPTER ELEVEN

"Shouldn't we be choosing our scent?"

Pre-Life: Jade & Voyor look at an aquarium

ONE OF MY favorite buildings in Pre-Life is Ocean-View. Standing as a monument to the diversity of species that reflects the history of World-Side, I always enjoy its splendor. By virtue of a simple voice command, I can observe the transition from any time period in a matter of seconds. The timeless perspective has always allowed me to honor the power and perseverance of nature. Today is no different as Jade points to the bubbles rising slowly from the stones at the bottom of an aquarium saying, "Aren't bubbles the perfect form of reflecting life in the moment?"

I'm taken off guard by the expectation of having to answer while, instead, concentrating on Jade's joyful face. She looks back at me and laughs, "The bubbles, the bubbles, focus my friend!"

With that, I turn my focus back to the dancing

flow that gently glitters and reflects all that they pass on their journey.

Jade continues, "Think of the stones at the bottom as the past and the air above the tank as the future unformed. The bubbles are our moment to move from past to future. Each is a moment. Each is a gift. Each is our present in the passage of time. Look closely, first they are related to the rock upon which they were born or in this case formed."

"Look at that one," she says as she points to a flat rock. "Because it is formed on a history that is solid and stable, the bubble grows to be quite large. Yet those over there, forming on that sharp rock, are quite small."

Voyor asks, "Why is the size important?"

"The larger the bubble the more character or mass it can hold. Like our lives on World-Side, our present moments can be small and unrelated, or quite richly filled with reflections of the past gone by."

World-Side: Ease holds the champagne flute

Ease holds the champagne flute up so that it is backlit by the rising moon as Chance says, "It won't be long now."

In my mind's eye, I see a montage of Leah since that first day of college. I see her face smiling, laughing, thoughtful and sad. Yet, she is always filled with a passion of being. Still, something pulls me to glance at the image of Grace, the woman that captures my imagination. With champagne in one hand and the newspaper in the other, I struggle to find a balance.

Chance states, "We've almost arrived at the front of the museum."

My heart begins to pound. The champagne is all but gone now as I set down the glass and release the paper to hold my hands together and focus. As birthdays go, this has become my most dynamic and yet it has not even begun!

The town car stops just short of the red-carpet area and is greeted by an attendant. Chance hands him some papers to inspect. A long moment later, they knowingly smile at each other and the attendant motions a guide forward to the car. The guide opens my door and greets me with a smile saying, "Happy birthday, Ease! Please follow me."

I exit the car and say farewell to Chance. I'm pleased to see that we're parked slightly away from and invisible to the crowd of press. There frenzy builds as each car delivers dignitaries, and the rich and famous.

With the focus over there, I have a certain calm and joy about not being part of that moment and instead being in my own. The guide slowly leads me up the stairs and away from the entrance, when suddenly the frenzy breaks into a roar! It is not the noise that moves me to look back but rather a wave of emotion that now rolls over me. My body tingles, yet I don't know why. I am numb with excitement. Every cell in my body begins to long! But long for what?

The guide, noticing that I have stopped, returns to my side and whispers, "That's her. That's Grace."

The speaking of her name flashes me back to her picture in the paper and then to so many years ago when I was captured within her gaze. Now, again, I find myself somehow lost. I am lost in a montage through the history of time. The Renaissance, Egypt, and places beyond this world dance and flash faster and faster in my head only to be broken by soft words, "Ease, we must go now."

I snap back to the moment to see Grace exit her limo lit by hundreds of flashes from the photographers' cameras surrounding her. Although I'm aware that I must move on, I choose to linger just a moment longer.

World-Side: Grace exits the limo

I'm thrilled to have arrived at this day as Marshal reminds me to allow the press a few extra shots. I've learned to look beyond the sea of flashes and connect with someone afar; a special soul that quietly wishes to know me. A soul, beyond fame and fortune, that ponders my name. Looking up slightly, I can't help but notice the full moon as it radiantly begins to fill the sky.

Suddenly, a wave of energy surges into me. In a void of frenzy, I am taken. Is this simply my ego demanding due course, or my heart still aching for love not found? Slowly, as if time stands still, I scan the crowd but don't know why. Then I'm at a loss for what I've wanted to see for so many years. I see a soul as radiant with love as me. My eyes can only see the glow of his soul, so near but far away. I see a soul whose quiet heart yearns to turn my night into day.

Marshal has seen this look before and whispers in my ear, "Grace my dear, it's time to go. We must move away from here."

The first step is the hardest as I ascend the stairs to share my vision of love, yet I still do not understand the basis of my own.

World-Side: Ease watching Grace

As I watch Grace take the first step up the stairs, I feel the guide gently press me forward and, on my way, again. As the path moves me farther away from the crowd, I finally turn away and renew my focus to be in my now. Slowly and whimsically, our path winds through a maze of gardens lit only by torch lights. The fragrances begin to dance in my head to a memory I can't seem to hold. I stop for a moment and gaze at the moon, hoping it will guide my way. Quiet and steady it shines back at me urging me forward with no further delay.

Pre-Life: Jade takes Voyor's hand

Jade takes my hand and guides me away from our bubbly friends, out of the building and into the adjacent gardens. As the sea is represented within, it is also here in the form of shrubs brilliantly sculpted into waves of flowers for all to see. Jade feels the scent of a nearby flower and asks, "Have you chosen our scent?"

Instantly I answer, "Shouldn't we be choosing our scent?"

Jade stops and gazes into my eyes with wonder at receiving an unexpected surprise. In the next moment however her face turns to fear saying, "Us? Us? I'm so very afraid that the hope of us is merely a charade! That this is all a heartless attempt of egos!"

Looking back into Jade's eyes, I feel her fear ebbing and flowing from heart to head and back again. She doesn't know me nor I her. Yet the season of us must be explored.

In the next moment, Jade breathes in deeply and breaks away in a skip. She skips first to one flower and then to another, smells each deeply and then moves on. I follow her path and carefully explore each scent as I watch her look with hopeful joy to find our signature.

Up ahead, I see her stop, spin around and fall to the ground giggling and laughing with a child's delight. In the same moment, my senses are captured by a distant fragrance that seems to penetrate my thoughts, my being, and my heart. I slowly move forward and then look down to find myself in a wave of lavender roses! With each shift of the breeze, I too am moved. My senses are full yet I long for more as I take a young bud and gently hold it near.

The flow and softness of petals guide my fingers. It calls me to share as Jade skips back with both hands full of roses in every color. In a moment of joy, her hands present the multi-colored bouquet as a background to the single rose I hold in my hand.

Jade, glowing with glee, laughs, "Oh perfect, you have found the color missing from my heart. You have found the scent of my song and the skip in my step."

She holds up six different roses to frame mine and I am struck by the rainbow of color. I exclaim, "We have found our union. Or has it found us?"

World-Side: The guide continues to lead
Ease up the path

As the guide continues to lead me through the gardens, I cannot help but remember the many scents as we pass. Each seems to tug at my heart and then makes way for the next, like peeling away the layers of fear from my heart's longing embrace. Our path leads us to the rear of the museum and far from the frenzy of tonight's social event. I now stand at the outside entrance of the arboretum, gently framed by arched trellises of vined flowers. The lights within are dim and designed to hold a mystery of what waits there.

The guide stops and turns to me with a knowing I do not share. She straightens my tie, gently smiles, and softly says, "Be not afraid of love's true moments, for they are the present for a heart not whole." She looks at me one last time and then slips into the night.

World-Side: Entrance of the arboretum

The roar of my beating heart surrounded by the silence moves me to tears. I ask the moon as it looks down on me, "Why am I so fearful? How can this be?"

I am, in this moment, filled with hopeful fear as the pulse of time echoes through my body. Slowly, so slowly, I reach for the door as if lifetimes pass between each second. But before I can grasp the handle of my future, it opens before me. The door has opened, yet there is no one to see. I've nothing to do now but walk into my present, carried so gently by the fragrances within.

Ahead, in the near distance, are candles longingly calling me closer. My fear gives way to a desire to be. My spine grows long and finds a new balance of power. Those candles, that a moment before spoke of darkness, now serve as a beacon by which to safely navigate back to a long-lost heart. Yes, yes as always, our forever journeys always require an endless supply of steps.

World-Side: Grace reviews her notes

Grace confidently reviews her notes for the coming lecture. Yet she is still filled with a bit of dis-ease. Thinking, "I'm in the moment, the present of my soul, yet something is still amiss." Marshal knocks on the door, "Five minutes Grace. Five minutes to fame!"

I think of fame. Fame!? What does fame have to do with my ego's sense of now? I feel so close yet far away from my heart's true longing. I was all too haunted as I stood by the car with a feeling, I'd felt years before. A knowing that is beyond my own.

I begin to write on the lecture program from years ago: how did I get to this place and time? How can my heart be still? How many times must my heart pay for the crime yet never know the thrill? I wonder with all the lust of life if that man from the path yet breathes. Wondering too on a lover's behalf if he was truly meant for me!? For with the knowing that he exists, I'm bound by my own embrace. Of love, sweet love here and now, yet beyond the human race. Where are you? Where are you, my timeless friend? Have you come back once more to find the end? End of longing, end of hope, end of fear and a need to cope.

Marshal slowly moves to Grace's dressing room door and sees that Grace is deep in thought. He feels the smallest of tears find his eye and reflects on a heart that may be living a lie.

Finally, he gently knocks and enters the room saying, "Grace, it's time to go."

I put down my pen and look into the mirror. The woman I see holds back her tears yet spurs her heart to feel, that the love within her might soon be revealed!

CHAPTER TWELVE

...'the logic of emotion'

Pre-Life: Jade & Mara look up at the sky

JADE AND MARA look up at the sky and throw flowers in the air. Dancing and skipping effortlessly with neither one having a care. Jade falls on the ground and looks up at the sky as Mara joins her.

In the quiet of the moment Mara asks, "What are you going to steward into World-Side this time Jade?"

Twirling a flower in her hand, Jade speaks, "It's all about green for me this time around! For the first twenty-two years I'm going to play. Play and play and play some more!" Both souls giggle. "Then, while on a very special picnic with Ease, he'll challenge me to reapply my passion to something, to anything but boys! In that moment, I'll be looking at a flower just as I am right now. That is the moment I'll be inspired to champion a greener, cleaner world. I'll remember and access my mastery of chemistry and blend it with my love of nature, fueled of course with endless passion. That choice will also serve our contract."

"How so?"

Jade continues, "Our deal is for me to interact with him for two cycles of seven years prior to him reaching thirty-three, correct?"

"Yes."

Jade smiles, "Every time I get doe-eyed with Ease, no matter where we are or what we're doing, I'll get a call from the lab about some sort of progress. That call will snap my focus back to the greener world! What makes this even better is that Ease won't challenge the moment because he was the 'shifter' and awakener of my passion in the first place."

"For him, each time we get close to a kiss, he'll have an opportunity to master his integrity for honoring my passion for the earth above his own desire for completion!"

Pre-Life: The little secret

They both hug as Mara whispers, "Brilliant! Have you shared this with Voyor?"

Thoughtfully, Jade answers, "No. No I haven't. I was going to, but Senior took me aside. She suggested that not sharing would add even more to Voyor's exploration of choice."

Mara falls briefly into a timeless reflection of memories and then adds, "Wow, no remembering, no intuition, and no shift for him. He'll only have pure choice. That's so beautiful!"

The girls hug again as Jade asks, "How about you Mara? How will you share your love in World-Side this time around?"

Mara pauses for a moment and then begins, "I've found on my journey that the world can distract us from understanding the difference between love and emotion. As I move forward in my World-Side career, I will develop a concept called 'the logic of emotion.'"

Jade's eyes get very wide as she sits up saying, "I need to know more. Please guide me!"

Pre-Life: Emotional logic

Mara looks upon Jade with joy and responds, "Certainly, my friend. It all starts quite simply really. Imagine you are speaking with a friend. You effortlessly move from one topic to the next when you suddenly hit a cord in the other. You both begin to argue, which in turn creates an orb or ball of energy. This ball is an emotion frequency that evolves between the two of you. The more you argue the larger it becomes."

"Then, as often happens, you are interrupted before you can work out your differences. So, what do you do? What choice do you have in the heat of the moment? In a perfect moment, each of you could simply agree to disagree, hug, and move on allowing the ball of energy to simply fade back into the universal grid. However, that rarely happens. More often than not, your egos engage with the demand to be heard, to be acknowledged or to be right! So, you both divide the ball of energy in half and each of you store it within an emotional buffer somewhere in your body and walk away. Now, depending on how you personally view the type of emotion that was created, you'll store the energy in different places in your body."

Jade adds, "An example please."

Mara continues, "Sure. If for example, the energy was about guilt, then you might store it in the buffer in your shoulders. If the energy was more about fear, then you'd put it near your gut. If it was about hesitation, then you'd probably store it around your knees and so on. This is a normal approach to our evaluation process. Our bodies are designed for this kind of temporary storage of emotional energy."

"So now back to us. Let's say the next time you and I see each other we're at a party and we're both having a great time. Neither of us wants to dampen the mood, so we both choose to not address the old issue that we now carry. Privately, we both recall the disappointment and are aware of the magnitude of the emotion in that moment but again choose not to address the topic."

"All goes well until we bump into each other or are moved to entertain our egos in some way. Here we are again, within an emotional exchange. Again, we create an emotional ball of energy. The longer we argue the larger it gets. And again, we are reminded that this is not the place to engage so we stop again, divide up the energy and most importantly, we once again store it."

"What happens to the original energy?"

Mara, pleased with Jade's attention answers, "Perfect question! As we add the new energy to the old, the old gets compressed. Compressed energy moves slower. The slower it moves the denser it gets. If allowed to continue, the dense energy becomes disease to the body and then finally manifests itself into the full essence of disease."

Jade excitedly shares, "So this is just chemistry and physics?"

"Yes Jade, emotional chemistry!"

"But why do we, or rather our bodies, keep holding all this old energy?"

Mara continues, "For two very important reasons. First, our bodies are like soldiers. They take orders without question. If our mind says, 'Jump,' our body says, 'How high?' Our body will do whatever is requested if it possibly can. The second, more intriguing reason centers on a World-Side notion of intelligence and wisdom. Each time we come into World-Side, we desire to expand and share our knowingness of soul-based wisdom. For us to maximize each lifetime, we engage this intellectual drive to move us along as effortlessly as possible."

"Now the key to remember here is that world-based intelligence is a reflection of the ego. Remember when I said in the beginning that we wanted or needed to be right?"

"Yes," Jade says, following Mara's teaching.

"Well, being right is an attempt of one soul to share truth of knowingness. As souls, we all want to share our journey so that we all don't have to experience all things directly. In World-Side, that translates into a notion of right and wrong and the perspective that makes them different. In World-Side, it's always about the most effective way of manifesting our intentions."

"So, if I want to effortlessly be able to cross a river, intelligence or logic would dictate that I take the time to build a bridge. The flaw however is that we assume a common set of skills."

"I don't understand."

Mara smiles, "So you agree that if I speak to a hundred souls on this side of the river about building a bridge that I speak the truth and I'm in my heart of sharing?"

"Yes," Jade agrees.

"But what then do I do when you ask the same of me? You keep asking, 'Why a bridge. Why a bridge?' Finally, I say, 'Because I'm right. It's the fastest way!' And you say, 'No.' Within your truth you effortlessly fly to the other side!"

Jade laughs, "I can fly!"

"Yes Jade, you can fly! For all the rest of us the bridge is our truth but for you it's an unnecessary task."

Jade smiles with understanding saying, "So in that instant the two souls both spoke their truths yet neither could understand the other's perspective!"

"Yes! That's an example of why we hold on to that

emotional energy. The second reason we hold it is out of fear. If, for example, you and I are arguing about how one goes about teaching children, you might be drawn back to your own childhood. You remember a moment that stands out when you were embarrassed by your teacher for not doing your lesson."

"Perhaps the teacher made you stand up in front of the class and explain why you were unprepared! As a child, your self-esteem and choices are in question. That one moment might fuel your own unrealistic demand to never be unprepared again. Your ego is now hard wired and more empowered to always say, 'This is not enough! Try harder! Go faster! Go longer!'"

"Any topic or situation that involves effort now hits an emotional trigger that transcends all possibilities of self-love and satisfaction. So, in this case, you will hold onto all events in which your effort is in question until your ego determines that you are not at fault! Further, if you have no means to prove the intention or your effort, then you might never release that energy, but instead hold it up to yourself to remind you to avoid any situations like that in the future."

Jade shakes her head, "Wow, an ego gone wild because a child missed a lesson. So how would their body react to continually storing emotional energy related to effort?"

Thoughtfully, Mara continues, "It could go one of three ways. First, if they feel that they could never try hard enough, then each time they encounter a trigger event they would store the energy and reflect.

Store and reflect. Once they fill their entire body with emotion, the body has no choice but to increase its mass. With a larger mass, the body can now store a bit more emotion until it again reaches a saturation point and increases its mass again. We see many examples of that extreme on World-Side."

"The second extreme is to be driven by the notion of always being prepared. In this mode, the soul constantly projects information into the future of what could go wrong based on past experiences. His world is about contingency plans."

"But it's impossible to plan for everything in the world. It's designed that way."

Both girls smile as Mara continues, "Exactly, those souls will never allow themselves the joy of discovery or a moment of satisfaction. They not only negate the present by looking to the future, but they only look at the negative future of what could go wrong. A soul in this aspect of ego attracts the negative energy of what they fear to themselves. Like a fire that we continually add gas to, they'll eventually burn out. Sadly, these souls usually take everyone around them down too in a blazing contract."

Jade remembers, "I remember exploring that approach. I came into a lifetime wanting to master four life aspects in a very short time. I thought it would be fun to run fast and hard."

Mara queries, "How'd that work out for you?"

Jade slowly shakes her head, "It didn't! I ended up breaking a few contracts and died a horrible death only to have to go back to World-Side again in the next life and start the lessons all over again! How about you Mara? With all that love in your heart did you ever get caught up in the cycle?"

Mara takes a deep breath and replies, "Yes indeed, Jade. We all must eventually explore at least half of the dynamics of limits to be one with infinity, and I'm no different. For me, it was getting lost in another soul's potential. I was that teacher in first grade that knew in my heart that a little encouragement would kindle a soul to explore. Unfortunately, my passion to move, to ignite and to inspire turned out to debilitate and drive many to disease. It was a hard lesson for me to simply allow a soul their own perfect journey."

"I don't understand. How can you be passively supportive?"

"For me, it was my desire to share but not to hold what that looks like. Sometimes when we begin a discussion with another soul it takes three minutes. Sometimes it takes three hours and sometimes three lifetimes. The trick is to embrace the compassion of sharing and not the passion to share."

Jade hugs Mara, "That's so beautiful! So, what is the third aspect of unhealthy emotional storage you spoke of?"

Mara begins, "It's not just related to emotional storage but rather emotion itself. It is called a 'shift.' Shifting is a soul's safety net so to speak. It is a way of allowing ourselves the freedom to explore an aspect of mastery and yet salvage a life experience.

On World-Side, they use the story 'A Christmas Carol' to impart that sometimes it takes a tragedy in one life to break the spell of intention. For me, it was about contracting an auto accident at a prearranged time in my life if I had passed a point of knowing."

"As a teacher, I was full of pride about all those souls I had inspired. That same pride had blinded me to an equal number of souls that I had driven to dysfunction. One day, I was driving one of my best students to her home after school and passionately continued her lesson along the way. With my focus not in the present, we were hit by a truck. My student was killed, and I was left never to walk again. My whole life as I knew it was gone in a flash! Over, and over, and over again I played back that last moment."

"Slowly, over the next few years, I realized the error of my pride. At that moment I finally allowed myself true understanding, a magical event occurred. On that day, the younger sister of my passed student came to visit me. She brought flowers, a smile, and a shocking request. With her mother just outside my door, the little girl asked if I would be willing to help her with her math. She went on to say that her older sister had always spoken so highly of me. Tears rolled down my face as I took the flowers from her hand. The mother entered and we hugged and that began my new life's focus."

"The girl came to see me now and again and soon others followed. Each would bring me a gift of sorts as a token of my sharing. My life became a series of moments. My joy grew as I embraced the art of being present and my life became an understanding of compassion."

Jade hugs Mara for a very long time. In that moment Jade whispers, "I love you!"

Mara replies, "I know."

CHAPTER THIRTEEN

... "*Your now is nearly here...*"

***World-Side: Grace gazes into the mirror
with quiet anticipation***

A FEELING OF knowing becomes me as I quell my floating fears. Fate has brought me to this point as well as my choices. The time is now to share my love and change the world again.

Marshal knocks lightly on my open door and asks, "Are you ready, Grace? Are you ready for love?" I look into the mirror seeing his smile and feel his heart's embrace. He's loved me from afar all these years yet has never made his case.

Marshal brings in more flowers asking, "Where would you like these?"

"Over there with the others."

I glance back through the mirror and notice one of

the arrangements is composed entirely of a rare rose grown only in Maui.

"Wait Marshal. Put those lavender roses here on my table."

He does so and moves to bring in the rest. Over a hundred arrangements fill the dressing room, yet my gaze has been captured by the one sitting before me. I gather the fragrance to me and breathe in deeply. I touch the young petals and then move to read the card. Be still my beating heart. My mind races to know who sent this token. Yet I fear it might only be a friend. Where is my knight? Where is my child? Where is my heart's longing for joy?

World-Side: Grace flashes back to the limo

Suddenly, I flash back to the museum entrance and getting out of the limo. The scene unfolds in slow motion. This time it allows me to see out between the beats of my pounding heart. There, far to the right and above the crowd, is a soul with a glow I've seen before. Years have passed, yet none it seems, since a lecture long ago. Could it be that light, so pure, is my long-lost soul? Could it be that moment in time when all is well within my world?

Seeing me drift, Marshal asks, "Are you ready?"

His words break the spell and bring me back to the card in my hand and roses I'm coming to know. Carefully, I open the card with wishful hope. I look with longing wonder as it simply reads "Your now is nearly here…"

Pre-Life: Jade & Mara hold hands

Jade and Mara hold hands and spin about until they fall to the ground in a pile of laughter.

"Teach me more about love, Mara."

"Teach me more about passion, Jade."

They sit up in front of a rose bush that bears one hundred lavender roses. Both girls breathe in the fragrance as Mara begins, "Emotion is about flow and movement from within. In a healthy way it allows us gifted moments. They are perceived moments that lie beyond our physical senses."

"Yes, I know that. Passion can also be the foundation of knowing if we can allow it to be free."

Mara continues, "And like passion, love is about the faith to simply be. We can't hold it or touch it, yet it can always be shared. It's the perfect light when we forget and are frightened."

Jade smiles, "Passion is always within the present. It allows us to take the next step into the future. Fear, in contrast, does not move us forward but rather moves us away from our now."

Suddenly Jade is quiet as Mara notes the change in her. Quietly Mara says, "Let your heart speak, Jade."

Reluctantly, Jade begins, "How will Voyor choose between us? How can his heart know? What will guide him between passion and purpose to embrace his inner heart?"

Mara replies, "You asked the question my heart felt so very long ago when time for me was new. It was a time when all was possible, and love first knew of me and you. Alas, however, I do not know! What I do know is that I trust Voyor's process to be fair and true. I know that he will search his heart about us. He's sought truth throughout the whole of time yet as a poet he seeks the perfect rhyme. He will be true to himself, to me and to you! And that my dear is the foundation of our perfection."

World-Side: Leah looks back through the mirror

In a small room just beyond the arboretum, Leah looks back through the mirror at a stunning, vibrant woman. In shades of gold, her dress flows effortlessly as she looks closely at her face saying, "Just breathe Leah, just breathe."

My heart pounds as I take yet another moment before I do my best. It seems like just yesterday when my love was first foretold. Yet how could I know for sure about the passion meant for me. I open my purse and reach in to find a card that found me long ago. I look again now to see "The Lovers" intertwined in passion.

Suddenly, I am eighteen again and about to start college. A dear friend insists I get a psychic reading, but I feel like such a fool. Tarot, magic, and past lives gone by seem all too strange in this modern day. But here I sit in front of a young woman named Zune and the cards that reflect me. My reading covers a lot of information about my life. Inventions and helping the world seem a bit far-fetched but are hidden deep within me. I like to play, not save the world.

Zune says, "Focus is the key." Zune is kind as she speaks of my health. But youth has blinded me. She adds that my path can easily change when I find balance between head, heart, and body, simply learning to refrain.

Finally, she comes to speak of true love that every woman yearns to know. I can't help saying, "Do you see my prince?" Yet part of me is afraid. Zune gets quiet for a long moment and then pulls another card from the deck.

Finally, she breaks the silence, "You'll meet him as if he's in a tree. His smile will seal your fate. First friend, you'll be as you struggle to find yourself with a line of would-be mates. Yet, I see another woman here but don't see how or why. I wouldn't worry about her though, for she's beyond the need to care."

A wave of energy leaps up my spine wondering if this could somehow be true. A feeling deep inside of me seems to stir. I ask, "Do I know her now?"

Zune answers, "No but you seem to be one of the same."

Zune pulls one more card and sets it on top of the rest as she looks closely in my eyes. Thoughtfully Zune opens her hands and shares, "This deck is spent, it no longer serves. Please take this card, keep it close and your fortune will always be near!"

I don't know what to do as Zune speaks, "I am honored to serve you. May your passion guide your path and have a lovely day."

I never went back to her, though I think about it today. Could Ease be that lover of old? Could this be our day?

World-Side: The candlelight draws Ease near

Each step is met with another as the table's candlelight draws me on. Like a moth to the flame, I inch closer as if something to my heart is truly dear. My mind still wanders back to the limo and memories of a lecture of old.

In the next moment, I feel that Leah is somehow nearby. I remember calling Jonah in my darkest hours of despair when my heart longed for something more. To his credit, Jonah is always a friend. He listens quietly with calm. In the end, his words still echo, "She'll find you and then you'll be as one under a paradise's sun."

I know not why I wait for love. How could this serve me now? I'm not sure in this moment of what to feel or how. Yet suddenly, I stand before a beautiful table trimmed in silver and set for two. It's so perfect and pure in a timeless way.

Music serenades my heart as I gather myself. I find myself surrounded in a sea of flowers backlit so gently in the warmth of the candlelight. The table is perfect and the champagne chills as the sound of songbirds fill the night. I know this place from deep within me where hope begins anew. All is remembered beyond the now, of a long-forgotten time.

World-Side: "You've come far to be in this place"

As I'm suddenly aware of her energy, Leah enters the room. In another part of the museum wild applause can be heard. Radiant and loving, Leah slowly glides toward me. Never in a million years could I have enjoyed so much what my eyes do see! Her lips slightly tremble with hopeful anticipation as I dare to look at her. It is there that I am timeless and see a true reflection of what it feels to be a long-lost prize.

Her joy rolls over me as my fears begin to change. I reach out slowly to take her hand; suddenly I'm no longer afraid. I dance in her eyes as a moth to her flame! Gone now is my heart's ancient pain. Finally, she speaks to break the spell in a loving voice I know, "Happy birthday to you my dear. May your life begin in this moment and your past simply fade. May your heart know love and all its joy never to pretend again."

From nowhere, a waiter appears and seats Leah and then helps me find my chair. We sit in silence under the full moon's spell and feel the caress of a gentle spring breeze. Wondering, as I look at her now, how could I just begin to see? That a woman of such passion in every way can also embrace the love of me.

Applause again comes to our ears and brings us back as we smile. She declares again, "Happy birthday! You've come far to be in this place!!!"

World-Side: This is your night, Grace

In the grand hall guests yell and cheer trying to lure me out with love. That's so beautiful.

Marshal puts his arms around me saying, "This is your night, Grace! Remember how very far you've come! It's time to take the stage."

I take one last glimpse in the mirror, smile, and head to the stage. The host, having worked the room into a frenzy, now guides the room back down to a peaceful moment and simply says, "And now my dear friends, Grace!"

The audience stands in unison with not a dry eye in the place. I walk out from behind the curtain and feel an intense wave of energy embrace me. I am not even at the podium, yet I'm in a moment filled with the fragrance of anticipation. The crowd's love meets me and sways. I embrace its signature and command the podium to me. The love I feel is pure and honest as I watch the audience finally take their seats.

I look at every soul, seeking that face. The one I saw years ago far from this time and place. Where is he? I see him not. I feel as though I've waited a billion years yet seem to be forgotten! A quiet now takes over the room to frame my very first words. Maybe love won't find me today but still it must be heard.

So, I take a filling breath and all at once begin, "Love is pure to share by all, but emotion does us in! We are so very specialized these days on what to watch, what to eat, what to say and of course how to feel. I offer a brief story to make my point. Say the phone rings and your closest friend has just been in a car accident. They rant about fault and blame and fear. Now, you know anything short of pure empathy would make you less than a friend, so you commiserate with them and for hours in the future to come. We've all been there playing the role of the best friend. Sharing emotions to what is most times the bitter end."

The audience mutters in agreement as I continue, "What we, as friends, rarely get is the 'back story' to the tragic moment. What we don't know is that two weeks earlier your dear friend realized that they couldn't afford the brand-new car they just bought. Each night they would cry out to spirit, not knowing what to do. Still too, you're unaware of a quiet man whose daughter just gave birth to a son. As a grandfather for the very first time, his worries are many. Happy but poor, his concern now focused on the junk he called a car. Wanting only safety for his new grandson, he too shared the moment of the accident. No blame could be found. No one is hurt. No fault to take. Spirit is just guiding the way. In the end, both souls get their answer. The grandfather gets a newer, safer car to chauffeur his grandson and your dear friend gets an affordable car."

"So now we can ask what about you? What will

you do with all the emotion you generated in social empathy? What will you do with that emotion you stored? Sadly, probably nothing! Understand that your friend and Gramps both experienced a moment of closure. A special moment, when with prayers unseen, they can knowingly release the trauma of built-up expression. Whereas you offer them congratulations on their new car and move quickly to the next topic of the day. Where is the yell? Where is the sigh? Where is your release?"

The audience's silence is broken by a woman's yell as the place bursts into laughter. I smile, "You can do better than that!" The audience begins to yell.

I continue, "Louder! Louder! Let it all go!"

World-Side: Sound breaks the mood for Leah and Ease

Suddenly the noise of a thousand yells breaks the mood for us. The noise is so odd that we can't help but laugh. I motion to the waiter and ask, "What's going on?"

The waiter shrugs and pours the champagne.

I begin, "Leah, I can't believe you did all this! This is way over the top. I'm only thirty-three."

Leah responds, "Oh silly you! With all your love and care for everyone else, it's time for you to receive!"

I flash back to the picnic and smile realizing my words then have been echoed back to me as the noise from the Grand Hall begins to fade.

World-Side: "You are here to evolve"

Grace continues, "Passive empathy is one of the silent killers of our age. We no longer have the luxury to simply turn away. It's time for us to be selective in what we feel and what we do. You must rise and defend your soul's purpose! You are here to evolve! You are here to expand! You are here to explore! You are not here to mourn the loss of moments gone by! For each time you think of what might have been, you again lose what can be. Trust your soul to grow rich in each moment and release your mind's need to reflect! Your mind is designed to report your journey. Your present is intended to be lived!"

I stop a moment to take a sip of water as the audience settles back into their seats. I continue, "Ok, let's jump back into our daily lives to a typical day. You come home from work and maybe watch the news. As the sensationalism of the broadcast fills the screen, you only hear the bad news. A murder here, a famine there, another scoundrel too. Part of you wants to be part of change and the other part says, 'What can I do?' The sadness here is that you generate guilt, indifference, or both in the form of emotions. And rather than using those emotions to fuel your actions, you simply store them away. We see how years of passive storing drains our youth and turns our hopes to fears. So please go home tonight with a new understanding of the aspects of emotions. In their pure form, they can motivate us to move forward. In their highest of purposes, they can save lives, reach to distant planets, and express the very heart of humanity."

"At their worst, they can surround our fears with a barrier that knows no equal and defies that same impassioned heart. Be selective, so selective of generating this fuel. But when you do create it, make use of it in the now. Because really, it's the only thing to do! So, as you go out each day surrounded by acts and passion gone astray, remember that you always have a choice. A chance to measure if and when to generate and/or store the emotion you've created. Because, as the song says, 'Things are only as important as we want them to be'!"

The audience erupts with applause that again fills the hall and echoes throughout the museum.

World-Side: Damn her cell phone!

Leah raises her glass and I do as well. She offers a toast, "To you, to me, to us! Happy birthday!"

For some odd reason the sound of our glasses coming together makes me aware of another place. It's as if I'm in both places at the same time. The bigger question is, where is *there*? I feel as if Leah is in slow motion as I take a step back from our celebration. What Leah has done tonight is extraordinary, but as for us, I just don't see it. As much as I've wanted her and longed for her touch, her passion always rules the day. I've come to hate her cell phone which always calls her away. Part of me is undone in each moment, feeling it will soon ring and again my heart will be on hold. This has got to end soon, or my heart will become cold.

Yet, she feels so right, in almost every way, to the soul I so long for. I remember the very first time I fell and there she was to see. I needed someone to kiss in that moment, like an angel from above. I'm returning to her now and am curious to hear her words. Something seems different now, but it's impossible to know.

Leah begins, "I've thought about us a lot these days and what you mean to me. I'm also aware of how my work has kept us apart in so many ways. You are and have been my first and only friend. The thought of being alone has scared me into thinking we might soon end. You have been there for me in the middle of the night when I was feeling so very scared. Yet you always know how to calm me with your gentle words and tone. That's why I've brought you here tonight, so that we can walk through another door, a door of hope, a door of truth, a door yet unknown. A door we can walk through together, with my hand to hold."

At that moment, I hear the crowd again in a distant round of applause, wondering how much I've dreamed Leah's words from lips that serve her cause.

World-Side: The lecture is complete

In the Great Hall, I watch as the audience begins to allow their new freedom to take hold. They now have a new way of looking at the world. It feels fun each time I give this speech to be the focus of so much joy from people that have lost their way in stressful times like these. I notice from the corner of my eye Marshal motioning for me to add, "I thank you! Thank you so very much. I'm so honored to share."

My task is done! This group of souls, like the ripples in a pond, is now moving to pass this experience along to all that are willing to hear. Refocusing on the audience, I share "I'll be taking a few moments to myself and then I look forward to meeting you in the Freedom Reception Room. Thanks again!"

The applause finally fades as I collect my notes and watch the guests leave the hall.

It's easy, yet hard, to see the spectrum of auras that don't complement me. I've often wondered in quiet times, how I know so much of love yet miss its rhyme.

Marshal meets me with a hug saying, "You found their hearts again! How much time do you need before you begin to mingle?"

Marshal's question seems different tonight yet always with the same words.

I respond, "I'm not sure my friend, but too long would seem absurd. I just need some time to myself to reflect what I've just done."

Marshal adds, "Like always, you have the walk of the place. I'll just buzz you if the crowd gets restless."

I hand Marshal my notes, look into his eyes and ask, "Where can I go to see the moon?"

Marshal has seen my look before and yearns to hold me tight, yet true to form, he quietly suggests,

"The arboretum in the west wing should serve you on this very special night."

World-Side: Grace wanders the halls

I sign a few urgent autographs from the front of the stage and then slowly find an exit. The sound of the world slowly fades away as I plunge into my heart. Why can't I find true love? Where is that soul that torments me so? He's here, I saw him. Yet he wasn't present for me!

I'm not sure where I'm going as I wander from room to room. Passing the various historic displays make me feel like I'm going back in time. Let's see, the 1800s in the U.S., the 1600s in Europe, and Egypt. Each time affects me in a strange way, yet it feels like a known comfort. It's like a thousand lifetimes call me to be one, yet it is one that I don't long to be! My heart yearns rather to be a part of a union of we!

I'm brought to my now with a tingling in my feet. It matches my heart in a familiar way that slowly moves me forward. I find myself at a junction, a crossroad of halls. I can go left. I can go right. I can simply move ahead. Yet now a fear begins to build within me. What if I choose the wrong path now? How will I really know the path to my heart's happiness? Which path to knowingly go? I've been here before, this funny place between head and heart and time. Urgency demands decision, yet no answers come to me. My head says this, my heart says that. What is a woman to do? But now I'm blessed with another's approach that gives me hope anew. My quiet heart is full of hope for a lover just for me. My head recalls memories of choices not yet known.

It's time to listen clearly to what my soul wishes to declare. Oh, wise and gentle knowing guide help me find my way. Quiet! Quiet, of my body I do plea. Forward. Forward, take a step and ask again, I hear. I will lead you to your love if you follow me in faith. I'm stiff with doubt, yet long to move as my feet lead the way. As much as I'm present now, this doesn't feel like me. Still forward I go with the smallest steps and there do I behold a faint glow of candlelight hints of a future yet untold. I must be dreaming wishful thoughts of guiding lights right now. Yet I look again as it gently calls to me. This seems so right beyond my whys, yet still brighter it does get. Now it begins to reveal an aura of the soul I've never met.

World-Side: Grace: My soul answers no more!

I stand before a doorway, now not sure of the course I took. I feel the moon's light shine down as if in a romance novel. Sweetly, silently my eyes do gaze upon a couple there. They're sharing a candlelight dinner with a moon's heavenly light. I look at her and then at me. We seem to be one and the same. I know I've seen her somewhere before as I look upon her. I see her aura and her being moves me from my present moment.

Drifting a bit, I remember how I saw her that very same day that I saw him for the first time. I remember those hands that blinded him and then whisked him quickly away. So long ago that strange day was, yet how can this now be? These are the same souls in a toast that sit in front of me.

I am frozen again in so much fear, yet my hand moves toward the door. I cry to my soul, "Please stop!" My soul answers no more! The knob turns and the door moves open in a gentle silence. Another step taken and I'm standing in a garden of the world's sacred space. The man I longed for now sees me and freezes. The woman turns slowly to see the expression on my curious and cautious face. The moment beyond time and space is now upon us, a moment full of hope and fear, a beginning, or a fall.

World-Side: Are you lost?

The silence seems unbearable with no one able to speak. Ease thinks, "It's her; it's her!" as he slowly rises and smiles.

As Grace moves forward, she thinks, "It's him; it's him," and a glow comes over her face. As Grace approaches, Ease asks, "Can I help you?" as their eyes finally meet! I feel as if I am taken with the whimsy of her eyes. The closer she gets the more my eyes expand, yet the less I really see. Is this an angel or a woman of the world?

Grace smiles and responds, "This is truly a

surprise. I was looking for the moon and found my way here quite unexpectedly. I'm so sorry to interrupt. It's been a very long and eventful day."

Still unable to break my gaze of her, I share, "My friend and I are also admirers of the moon. I am Ease, this is Leah, and there is the moon upon which you dwell."

Overwhelmed by the moment of our gaze, Leah excuses herself and quickly slips away. She has found herself at a loss for words for the first time in her life. From the safety of a nearby door, Leah watches Grace and Ease in touchless embrace. With words beyond the ways of the world, their auras grow to fill the place.

World-Side: Grace and Ease first words

Grace turns her gaze to the moon and allows me to do the same. I look at the moon and then back into her eyes. Deeper and deeper I begin to fall saying, "Do I know you? It seems so... but how and when did I first hear your call? Perhaps a million or a few years ago it's really hard to say."

Grace responds, "I go by Grace. A million years maybe! But it's good to see you now!"

We smile and laugh like dear old friends but I'm at a loss for something to say. Then movement from the corner of my eye again breaks my gaze. Before me, I witness butterflies surrounding Grace's form. She opens her arms and hands to receive them now like a child of nature's glow. My heart holds its breath and I move closer to her, while butterflies gently float by. Now she is almost covered with only a few still choosing to fly.

"You seem to have a way with them. How do they trust you so?"

"It probably has to do with my heart's yearning to be in this moment's flow."

I desire to move forward again but know I cannot, for this moment is beyond this place. But as the last of those words leave my thoughts, the butterflies begin to swirl. First, they fly around her and then include me. I'm blinded by the sight as my inner child beckons. Closer, still closer we both inch towards each other. Our bodies lead us on. We almost touch in a strange but familiar way. I am no longer able to move forward, no matter how I try. A force beyond all my passion won't let me go.

I, Grace, look at him, now face to face. We silently raise our hands as if to begin a hug. An embrace that reflects a thousand loves; a thousand hearts that beat as one. His aura blinds me in a thrilling way. I know my life has just begun. I love and fear the moment at hand as my soul's reasons slip away. I dare to come into his knowing, yet to find my way.

In stillness, our hands have stopped but a moment apart. We begin to fill the room. I reflect on our steadily beating hearts, for it is from them together that our journeys have been traced. Energy now flowing between us, my edges fade away. No longer able to see with eyes, I'm taken by his ways. Gentle, yet strong, he stands before me, defying all my fears. Yet untouched, we have been the closest of unrelenting peers.

World-Side: Leah returns

Motionlessly Leah senses as their auras create a sweet flow. A single cloud begins to hide the moon, yet it does not diminish the full brilliance of their glow. Within me, I feel them but I'm not sure how. Perhaps it's a longing for what they're having that almost makes me cry.

As if pushed and pressed to move forward, Leah and the moon return to the room. Grace and Ease lower their hands and step beyond the moment.

Leah comments, "I've never seen butterflies so playful. To fly in circles around you, it's like they're on some sort of a parade."

Grace shares, "They've been my friends since I was a girl. They love to follow me so." Then Grace gently moves her hands and watches them move to go.

"I'm so sorry to alter your evening," Grace confides.

Ease replies, "It was really no bother at all."

With a forced smile Leah adds, "Looks like new times are in store and you heard an angel's call."

Looking slowly from Leah to Grace, I add, "You see tonight, whatever we do is a joyful present for me! For it's my birthday! So, join us now in a toast to new friends, the moon, and roses in bloom!" The waiter magically appears and pours champagne for all of us as we take in the moment and drink to new and old friends with feelings of renewal.

World-Side: A toast by three

As if painted with magic, the moon shines down on three radiant souls. Two are angels framed in a garden of light, love, and life. As for me, who really knows? Life's fickle game has matched a lifetime of quiet longing with infinite choice! Knowingly we stand before each other; all lost in the moment. Yet within that moment, Grace stands in the richness of her own glow, Leah vibrates a harmonic song of gleeful passion, and I rekindle a notion of a heart that yearns to know.

Glasses three held to the heavens that bubble in the night. Each of us wonder from deep within, how could this feel so right? Old friends and new now share a moment to celebrate with me. For I have come so very far to now be thirty-three!

CHAPTER FOURTEEN

"Now what?"

World-Side: "What a déjà vu."

GRACE IS THE first one to break the silence after sipping some champagne. She looks closely at Leah and declares, "Your energy is extraordinary. I've never seen anyone with such clear and passionate centers!" Ease laughs, "Then you haven't looked in a mirror lately because you two could be spirit twins!" Leah asks, "What do you mean?" Ease continues, "It's amazing how similar your auras are. As an intuitive healer I am blessed with the ability to see auras. You both have almost identical auras from top to bottom. It's just amazing!"

Leah responds, "Well, I can't see auras, but I can definitely feel the energy you are both emitting! Wow, you're off the charts! Are you sure you don't know each other?" Just then a bell can be heard from another part of the museum. Grace responds, "Oh, that's for me. I hate to cut this short, but I have fans to attend to." Ease remarks, "That's where I know you from. It was a lecture a few years ago. I was standing in line to meet you and a fire alarm went off."

Grace reflects, "Great memory." Grace now looks at Leah and recalls, "You were there too, if I remember correctly! Wow, that was years ago, and here we all are. What a déjà vu. We must get together again soon. Here is my card. Happiest of birthdays to you!"

Grace quickly exits the room leaving Ease and Leah in an awkward moment of silence. Suddenly, Leah's phone vibrates to reveal a text message from her lab. She looks back and forth at Ease and her phone and finally says, "Damn it! I have to go now. I have to go right now. I'm so sorry! I'll make it up to you. I'll catch up with you as soon as I can. Love ya!" And with that she exits the room. Ease slowly sits down and stares at the bubbles in his champagne glass while picking up one of the roses from the table and embraces its fragrance. In the next moment, a single butterfly lands on the rim of his glass. Disappointed, he looks at the butterfly and says, "Well, I guess it's just us tonight."

World-Side: You must be special

The next day Ease impatiently looks at his cell phone and notes the time. Muttering to himself, he says, "I've called Leah three times today with no response."

I guess it's time to try Grace. She answers immediately. The tone of her voice is like an angel. After a few minutes it's obvious that we need to meet again as soon as possible. Grace suggests we meet at the museum again since she has spiritual coaching sessions booked with a few souls from last night's lecture.

I show up at the museum a few minutes before our appointment and check in with the front desk to meet with Grace. The woman at the desk immediately smiles saying, "Wow, I see you have just been added to the top of Grace's waiting list. It's well over a hundred souls and still growing! Sadly, she's only got time to meet with ten souls. But, hey you're one of the very lucky ones!" I respond, "Yes, I truly do feel blessed, thanks." The woman, still smiling, directs me to sit in a waiting area just off the main gallery. As I wait, I can't help but notice how happy everyone seems to be. Thinking of Grace, my mind wanders to recall the times our paths had almost crossed. Knowing that we are going to meet in a few moments feels like a dream.

Suddenly a surge of energy rolls up my spine and I see Grace hug an older woman who is in tears. Grace lifts her chin and looks directly into her eyes saying only, "You are love. Now go and make the world a better place." A feeling of calm comes over me as Grace turns toward me and our eyes meet! I am lost in her gaze, and I find myself moving toward her. In our next moment, we cannot be any closer and still not touch. I blurt out, "Wow, your energy is extraordinary! It was truly a delight to watch you transform that woman's fear into a focused hope and joy!"

Grace acknowledges, "It's certainly nice to talk

to someone who can actually see the results of my work. Have you been waiting long?" Ease, responds, "No, not really." Grace smiles and shares, "Oh good, I was afraid I would hold you up. I just had three back-to-back sessions and I'm quite saturated." Ease smiles, "I totally know what you mean. Do you need to reschedule?" Grace firmly responds, "No! Absolutely not. I've will not let my tendency to overbook my schedule affect my ability to meet with you today." Ease offers, "Can I make this any easier for you?" Grace smiles, "Would you mind walking and talking? Ease smiles back, "I'd love to. Do you have any place in mind?" Grace happily suggests, "I know a perfect section of the museum that I wandered through last night on the way to discovering you!" Ease smiles, "Sounds perfect. Shall we go?" Grace points forward saying, "Yes let's!"

We headed toward the Historic Timeline corridor map. It shows how the matrix is laid out within time and global location. As we walk slowly forward, we find ourselves in Virginia just before the beginning of the Civil War. Grace stops to read one of the placards that describes the bravery of many souls to teach African Americans, both free and slaves, to read and write.

Grace, almost in tears, says, "I'm having such an intense déjà vu. There was so much pain and fear around the act of teaching during this time!" Ease adds, "Yes, in my mind's eye, I'm seeing fire all around us." Grace looks at the next placard that reads that a group of five hundred Confederate soldiers burned down the entire town of Hampton during the beginning of the Civil War. Even in the face of destruction, teachers and students alike were not swayed from their determination for education. On September 17, 1861, the first classes were held on the grounds of present-day Hampton University, under what became called the Emancipation Oak.

Ease shakes his head and declares, "This is so crazy! It's like I can feel you now and then at the same time. Is there such a thing as a group déjà vu?" Grace responds, "Well if you think about it, there must be group experiences if you believe in soul groups!" Both somewhat shaken, Grace and Ease slowly walk away from the 1800s and into the 1700s. The visit to this section is like the last as both Grace and I co-experience the highlights. However, our personal energy seems to be growing exponentially! The more we're together the more limitless our energy becomes.

Pre-Life: Jade, Mara and Voyor meet within the Temple of One

Voyor looks at the various wall hangings within the Temple of One that depict the results of what other soul pods have created. Each one a reality to behold. Jade and Mara slowly and quietly enter the chamber. Voyor smiles saying, "Thanks for meeting me here on such short notice. I'm sure you have many details to work out still. However, I am growing more concerned about your approaches to win me over in the last days of World-Side. It strikes me that you might deflect each other rather than invest in attracting me. You can't really approach each other's shortcomings because you have the same. It would be like fighting with your own shadows and I don't feel like that will serve you."

Jade says, "I can only go with what I know being new to your pod. I'm going to focus on my selfless compassion toward others rather than speak of myself. I must get you to remember that one moment of bliss doesn't guarantee that another will follow. The only truth is that we reside in the now." Voyor smiles, "Oh so very true."

Voyor looks now on Mara and asks, "And you, Mara, how do you view this tangled web of persuasion?" Mara reflects, "For me it is quite simple really. I know that every moment that we share and have shared is but half of the whole that binds us. I do not worry about that which has not come for I can only commit myself to this now and worry not about what lies beyond." Voyor reflects a moment saying, "I go now to prepare. Many thanks to you and your commitment to the whole to come."

World-Side: "I can use a break as well."

After visiting a few more eras, the intensity has started to wear on me to the point that I am about to ask Grace to take a pause. But before I can utter a word, Grace says, "Yes, I can use a break as well. How about we take a moment in the food court? I'm famished." I look directly at her and realize she is speaking from her mind and not her mouth! Shocked, I ask Grace, "Did you just read my thoughts?" Grace reflects for a moment and says, "Why yes, I guess I did. Wow, that was unexpected. Can you read mine?" I open myself in the next moment and listen through my mind's eye. Suddenly I hear Grace's soft voice repeating "We are one. We are one." I smile and say, "We are one!" Grace smiles saying, "Yes, we are!"

Quiet falls over us and we are silent for a long moment. The silence is broken when I hear Grace's thought saying, "I'm still hungry!" I laugh and think, "Me too. I'll get a couple of menus." As I approach the server behind the counter, I wonder how far away we can be and still be connected? I hear Grace's thoughts say, "I can still hear you." All through lunch, we playfully explore our newfound gift.

Out of the blue, my phone rings and I see that it's Leah. Grace looks up at the clock on the wall and realizes that she is almost late for her next consulting session. I hear Grace think, "I'm late for a session. Can we meet for dinner tomorrow?" In the same moment I say, "Hi." to Leah. Feeling a bit fearful, Leah says, "Can we meet for dinner tomorrow?" In my haste I blurt out "Yes." In the next moment, all is quiet as I reflect on what I've just done. Grace telepathically says, "I'll text you where and when to meet and I'll see you tomorrow. Thanks for a great afternoon!"

In the next moment, I refocus on Leah saying, "Is everything alright? What happened?" Leah gathers herself and shares, "There was an accident at the lab and two of my teammates were badly hurt. I stayed at their bedsides through the night and most of the day. I'm so sorry about your birthday dinner." Ease says, "I understand, I was worried about you. You sound totally exhausted, and we can catch up sometime tomorrow. Does that work for you?" Leah barely responds, "Yeah, that works, I need to get some sleep. But first, I need to check on a few things before the investigators inspect my lab. See you tomorrow."

Later that day I receive a text from Grace to meet the next evening at a quiet little restaurant downtown at eight-thirty. Then I text Leah to meet me at the same location at seven o'clock. That way I can have an opportunity to speak with Leah and still have plenty of time to meet Grace a bit later. I am distracted all day with yesterday's events replaying in my head. Wow, Grace and I can read each other's minds! My head just keeps expanding. I can barely get my head around it!

Pre-Life: Senior & Voyor Walk toward the Temple of One

In the quiet of the moment, Senior begins, "Voyor, may I ask you a question?" Voyor thoughtfully responds, "Of course, anything my dear one." Senior stops walking and simply queries, "What now?" Puzzled, Voyor says, "What do you mean?" Senior continues,

"Well, now that you have succeeded in qualifying two souls who both fully complement you, how will you choose? What will be your basis?"

Voyor quietly answers, "I've been so wrapped up in ensuring the perfect energy profiles that I really have yet to even define the type of relationship that would serve us. Thanks so much for bringing that topic forward into the light. Early on, Mara and I had several discussions about how to divide up various topics. One of the most complex was that of understanding what kind of relationship would serve both of us."

"We went round and round, back and forth. Every time we thought we were close, we would realize that one or both of us was in fact setting up a dysfunctional and unsustainable expectation. We also were unable to balance comfortable predictability with spontaneous growth. It was for that reason that we agreed to have Mara focus on that topic while I focused on the physics required to create and sustain complementary energy."

Senior askes, "So is having Jade in the mix helping or hurting the process?" Voyor smiles, "I wish I knew, but it's lost on me. Ironically, Jade would have a better knowledge of this topic than I do since she mirrors Mara's understanding. On a positive note, because Mara focused solely on that topic, she was able to create an entire career based on the science of love. I do, however, have a couple working theories."

"First, on face value, time seems to be the only universal currency that allows any kind of relationship to exist." Senior questions, "How so?" I continue, "On World-Side, relationships are measured on the length and quality of commitment to each other. So, if I meet a couple that has been together for fifty years, they are revered to have a successful relationship. It is also assumed that both members of that relationship continue to make countless compromises for the sake of the whole."

"On Pre-Life however, time is used to reference how long a soul navigates in a specific direction of self-full growth. Having said that, maybe time serves a bit of both." Senior asks, "How so?" I offer, "Perhaps a soul is meant to look upon an understanding from a selfish and selfless point of view simultaneously in this way they eventually find mastery from looking from the outside in and the inside out at the same time. Visually, it's like looking at the Yin-Yang symbol. We can focus on the light side with the dark dot or we can focus on the dark side with the light dot."

World-Side: Ease's core question

Grace and I have spoken of so many topics, but I find her breakdown of a typical couple fascinating. With that in mind, I carefully recall her understanding of the couple that has remained together for over fifty years. First and foremost, they both had careers which kept them apart for eight to ten hours a day. Next, we can subtract eight hours for sleep. In addition to that, we can add two hours of commute time. On top of that, add a few hours for home maintenance, food preparation, and of course interacting with family and friends. All this commitment leaves them with perhaps less than an hour a day for potential interactions. So, if they wish to invest some personal time in their spiritual growth, they are left with all but nothing.

Therefore, most of the spiritual growth only begins to occur after a soul retires. Which brings me back to my core question. Namely, what can a soul actually offer another soul to serve as a foundation for creating a relationship? I guess it's as simple as offering a consistent and compassionate interest in each other's spiritual journey. Without that focused exchange, we have nothing.

World-Side: Ease's reflects on conversations with Grace

I wanted to text Grace ten times during the day and thank her for getting me on the right track regarding so many topics, but somehow, I restrain myself. Last night however couldn't have gone any slower. My mind continued to float from one time period or topic to the next. And, in every case, I found myself in a relationship with Grace in some dynamic way.

I've sent texts to Zune most of the day and finally receive her response saying, "It's all wonderful that you want to support others, but what, my dear friend, do you want from life?" I've arrived at the restaurant a little before seven o'clock to meet with Leah. The place is very low-key and quaint, as advertised. It seems like the perfect place to gather my thoughts on my relationship with both Leah and Grace. I look at my watch and note the time to be almost seven forty-five. I can't help remembering all the times I waited on Leah during our college years. A minute later Leah texts, "I'm almost there." All I can do is shake my head.

In that moment, I realize the type of relationship I've been having with Leah and that I'm going to need Grace's help to sort it out. Because my time is quickly running out, I text Grace immediately to make her aware of what she's about to walk into and to ask for her support. Why do I really need to speak with Leah privately anyway? I don't feel guilty about the time I've spent with Grace. However, I feel frustrated with Leah in general. All those countless times we almost embraced. Over and over, time and again I found myself yearning for a taste of her endless passion, but I was left with nothing, nothing but broken hopes. I look up to see Leah come through the door and toward me without her usual smile.

As Leah approaches Ease, she feels confused. He seems to be not like his usual self. She wonders if Ease is still upset with her for having to leave his birthday dinner. Leah breaks the ice with, "Sorry I'm late, I just came from the hospital." Ease responds, "Is everything all right?" Leah, almost in tears says, "No, two on my team were badly burned in a fire in my lab trying to save our work." Ease shakes his head and says, "I don't get it, why would they do that?" Leah continues, "We've been working on a way to make plastic break down just like a piece of paper would in normal sunlight. Can you imagine how that could affect the state of garbage in the world?" Ease responds, "Yes and no, I guess. But what's that got to do with two from your lab team getting burned?" Leah, almost crying, "We got a little ahead of ourselves and skipped a few protocols while trying to isolate the active molecules. The formula is just so damn unstable. It's all my fault!"

Remembering some of the topics I engaged with Grace has provided me with the desire to dig deeper into Leah's responses and not to just accept her answers without challenge. Curious, Ease asks, "Where were you when this happened?" Leah responds, "Celebrating your birthday with you." Ease states, "Then you weren't even in the room. Why were you in such a hurry?" Leah shares, "There is another team in my field that has produced similar results and now it's a race to get published first. It could be the first trillion-dollar breakthrough of the millennium!" Ease draws a blank look saying, "And how long have you been trying to save the world?" Leah reveals, "Since senior year at college." Ease realizing a long-time mystery says, "Well that sure explains a few things!"

Leah now composes herself saying, "So, what's up? Why are we here?" Ease begins, "I've spent the last few days interacting with Grace which in turn has me thinking about what I want out of life regarding a relationship. I no longer feel that I can wait for you to be available to invest in me or our relationship. Just now, you helped me understand why I've been playing second fiddle to your career."

Just then, Grace walks in the door and is beautifully radiant. We connect eyes, then she acknowledges the owner and joins Leah and me at the table. By the look on Leah's face, it is obvious that she is surprised to see Grace walk in and join us.

Feeling both of us Grace asks, "May I join you?" I respond, "Please do." Grace calmly takes off her coat and joins the group. Confused, Leah asks, "Why is she here?" I begin, "I asked Grace to join us so that we might untangle our checkered past. After all, she does represent a unique take on the science of love." Leah, a bit taken aback says, "Whatever! I should be back at the hospital. The police are waiting for me to make a statement, so make this quick!" Grace smiles and asks, "Have you done everything you can for the situation there?" Leah counters, "Yes, I suppose so. What's your point?" Grace continues, "From what I've gathered from Ease, you are a master at being emotionally unavailable. Like right now for example, you state that you need to be at the hospital, yet you are not required to be there. The core of that statement is your use of a socially unchallengeable position to avoid any emotional interaction that you are unwilling to address in the moment."

Leah says, "Let me ask you a question." Grace smiles saying, "Certainly, go ahead." Leah continues,

"What do love, science, and relationships have to do with anything these days anyway? Maybe I've missed something, but I don't see any Mr. Wonderful on your arm. Or are you waiting for your soul mate? I mean really, what are you waiting for?" Grace knowingly smiles saying, "I'm not waiting at all. I made my choice a thousand lifetimes ago. I knew then that a twin flame is worth waiting an eternity for. Because anything less is the biggest lie one could sell to themselves." Leah laughs out loud, "That's a bit of a stretch don't you think?"

Grace counters, "I guess that depends on if you're looking to create a relationship or to avoid one! It's one thing to keep your options open, but quite a different choice to feed on the perpetual admiration of a hopeful soul. Don't you think it's time you cut bait with Ease and let him move on, or is this the moment that your phone is programed to ring?"

Leah stands incensed about what has just been inferred. Looking at me Leah says, "We'll talk later!" and walks out of the place. I look at Grace and say, "Well, that didn't quite go like I thought it would." Grace acknowledges, "I can't really say I'm surprised." I share, "I still love her so much!" Grace empathetically replies, "Yes, I get that. But 'do you like her?' is the more important question to ask yourself. Does she consistently honor you? Or are you her fix for emotional boredom? Remember Ease, without honor you have nothing. Without trust you have nothing. And without interest you have nothing." As I begin to understand Grace's wisdom, the waiter comes to the table and asks if we are ready to order. I laugh to myself, thinking, "We have already been served."

Unexpectedly, I receive an odd text from Leah that reads, "I think I'm being followed."

Pre-Life: Senior is approached by a Messenger in the Temple of One

Unexpectedly, Senior is approached by a Messenger. The Messenger speaks quietly in Senior's ear. The expression on Senior's face becomes very somber as he looks at Voyor saying, "Voyor, your insights will have to wait, a situation has developed, and I need your full attention." Voyor says, "What is it?" Coldly, Senior asks, "Voyor, when was the last time you saw Jade?" Confusedly, Voyor asks, "What do you mean? I was with her and Mara in this very space not a moment ago." Senior shares, "That is quite troubling!" Voyor asks, "Why so?" Senior notes, "Without Jade you have no choice and without choice you have no completion…"

World-Side: Something is amiss

After tuning into Senior's messenger in Pre-Life, Zune selects one of the decks from her shelf. Unfocused, she inadvertently drops the cards on the floor and is taken aback to see the whole deck facing down except for three cards. Zune remembers seeing these three cards often in readings for Ease and Leah. Death, The Fool, and Justice. The cards seemingly speak to her that something is amiss with Leah.

Pre-Life: What's going on?

Senior immediately leaves the Temple of One to investigate the news. Voyor, unable to contain himself, begins to vent. "What's going on? This selection process was not supposed to be this hard. I need to go someplace quiet where I can think. I must get back to the basics. First, it was just about Mara and me merging into a new reality and finding a spot to call home. Now, Jade is gone and reported missing from both Pre-Life and World-Side and for all intents and purposes I no longer can make a choice regarding my complement going forward."

"I feel like I want it to start over, go back to the beginning when it was pure and simple. However, now I am left with anything but a simple choice. I'm feeling that somehow, it's all about continuing to study the Yin-Yang symbol. On one hand you have a white tear with a black dot of doubt, on the other hand you have a black tear with the white dot of hope."

"It is both balance and perpetual simplicity of motion. I think the answer, however, lies in the line in between the two tears. It is that line that is neither the dark nor the light but simply the division between the two. Regardless of which side you choose to be. You can learn and grow from either side."

"Thinking now about Mara, and our approach to expand in a very balanced way, continues to haunt me. Can we eventually comprehend everything in the dark side by exploring everything in the light side? Which begs the question do I need to ever dwell in the light side, but simply embrace everything in the dark side to move forward and create my own unique reality?"

"Perhaps I am left with the notion that I don't need to choose between Grace and Leah; but in fact, choose both and neither at the same time. And in doing so, I can not only experience what both souls have to offer but also would gain the attitude and joy that defines each of them individually. Why should I choose only one of the two when clearly each one brings a different dynamic to the table? Friendliness aside, I have unquenched passion in everything that Jade brings to life. As for Mara, I can only begin to consider the possibility of comprehending her passion as well."

"Proposition, if I choose both, do I not gain everything even though my aspect of that would represent a disproportionate amount of energy and motion? What good is passion without the opportunity to reflect on experiencing it?"

"Proposition, what is the ability to recall if not supported by the ability to reflect on that experienced passion? I have invested hundreds and hundreds of lifetimes with the intention of manifesting the most efficient and effective way to create my reality, and in saying that now I realized the futility of such an effort."

"Resolved, whether an example to others or an adventure in the making, I am my own reality and will always be so regardless of what other information is available to me. Yet, I am still at a loss to understand how to qualify or verify various origins that come my way. I am in a space where everything that I hoped to be is already so and am moved to perpetually desire to grow. I find myself expanding, emoting, and reflecting in the dawn of my being."

"I am and will forever be the ever expanding me and to that end I am laughter, love, and light to the all that is me."

In a quiet moment, I look into a reflection pool and wonder how the seniors can watch passively as each soul reaches for an understanding of self without sharing their own trials and tribulations of working the path before us. It seems so evidently innocent to be on the other side of this understanding but also realize that in comprehending and owning this perspective is not a gift to share with any other soul. Because, in doing so would be enabling versus empowering that soul. In the end, it is our personal joy to watch each soul in their own time realized that foundation of their being and in doing so transcend the notion of now and forever. And so, it is…

Made in the USA
Columbia, SC
10 August 2022